A BOY TO REMEMBER

Books by

AMELIA ELIZABETH WALDEN

Gateway
Waverly
Sunnycove
Skymountain
Marsha On-Stage
Victory for Jill
A Girl Called Hank
All My Love
Daystar
Three Loves Has Sandy
I Found My Love
My Sister Mike
Palomino Girl
Today Is Mine
Queen of the Courts
Where Is My Heart?
A Boy to Remember

A
BOY
TO
REMEMBER

Amelia Elizabeth Walden

THE WESTMINSTER PRESS : Philadelphia

LIBRARY OF CONGRESS CATALOG CARD No. 60-11368

PRINTED IN THE UNITED STATES OF AMERICA

To
  CORINNE NEBIL
in admiration of her work as an
artist and her great zest for living

Sincere appreciation from the author
to

VIRGINIA E. PARKER

*Instructor of girls physical education
at Staples High School, Westport, Connecticut*

for sparking the idea of a Midwestern basketball novel
and giving generously of her time in the technical research

A BOY TO REMEMBER

KARIN BERGLUND gave a final tug to her safety belt as the jet airliner prepared to land. All around her, she felt the tensions of the landing. Fellow passengers stirred, fretted, braced themselves. A baby tried his lungs. His squeals and howls vied with the insistent hiss of the jet. A fit of coughing seized the man next to Karin. Somewhere behind her a girl laughed nervously. Above these sounds the calm voice of the hostess issued orders about safety belts.

Karin was not afraid of the landing ahead. Fear gripped her, but it was personal and far-reaching, a fear of the unknown, of what lay around the next corner of her life.

She looked out of the window of the jet, down upon the lights of the approaching city. Her thought was: The Midwest doesn't look much different from the East — from up here, anyway. That city below could be New York or Boston. But I wonder what it's going to be like when I run smack-bang into it.

She had been wondering this during the entire flight. A magazine lay unopened in her lap, and two books and a box of chocolates, the parting thoughtful tokens of her father and his new wife, were on the seat beside her. Nothing interested her. Nothing held her attention except the nagging worry of what her life was going to be like out there on the prairies.

The fact that this had been the least of three evils, and her own choice at that, did not lessen her anxiety. When her father had remarried, after a long widowerhood during which Karin had been the apple of his eye, she had been happy for him. Her father had met Joan, his new wife, at one of the advertising agencies for which he worked as a commercial artist. They had a lot in common, and Karin saw instantly that Joan was very much in love with her father. Moreover, Joan had extended a sincere invitation for Karin to live with them.

Karin knew that life in a New York apartment with her father and his new wife would not be the same as life had been in a cottage in Connecticut where she and her father had lived with a dog and a cat and a chronic brood of puppies and kittens.

Joan was sweet, but she was also orderly, systematic, and ambitious. The slapdash manner in which Karin and her father had lived, where friends and fun and visions and ski trips and paintbox jaunts and bull sessions at midnight were more important than clothes or elegance or bills paid on the dot, was a thing of the past.

So Karin had said no, she thought the newlyweds ought to be permitted to live alone, for a while anyway. They had offered her a choice of any girls' boarding school within budget bounds that she would like. She howled with outrage. "Me! Go to one of those pink-tea riding academies! Not on your life. If it's finishing you want to give me, I'll be finished some other way."

"Well then, Skeets," and her father's voice, caressing her nickname with the special persuasion that almost always won her over, "how about your grandfather's farm

14

in the Midwest?" She had been so choked with hurt and anger that she had been unable to answer. "They want you, Skeets. Your grandmother is lonely for young blood in the house. Your grandfather can give you a lot that I can't afford."

"I don't like the Midwest."

"You've never been there. How can you not like something you've never seen? The people are wonderful, warm, and friendly. They'd do anything in the world for you. They're sort of like the space out there, big and expansive. They have a generosity that bowls Easterners over. What's wrong with the Midwest?"

She had not answered him because he knew very well what was wrong with the Midwest. It was the same thing that had been wrong with it when he, a young art student, had pulled out in his late teens and come east.

It was her grandfather that was wrong with it.

Now, waiting for the jet's final swoop down upon the splash of light below, she shuddered again with apprehension.

Her remembrance of her grandfather, from the one visit he had made east during her childhood, was still vivid and electric. His towering frame, his booming voice, his swagger, his rolling laugh, the aura of excitement that surrounded him, these were things that fascinated, yet at the same time overawed her. Her grandfather did things on the grand scale, not so much to impress, but because he could not help thinking big. He was generous to a fault, handing out quarters and half dollars to her playmates.

Yet, behind the munificence was an iron will, a mind and character as strong and overpowering as the giant stature of the man.

He gave, but he expected also to be obeyed. Karin had felt this instinctively the first time she had put her hand

15

into her grandfather's big, work-hardened paw and let him lead her down the street to the corner store. He loved her very much. He would buy her anything. He was very proud of her, but he let it be known that she belonged to him.

"*My* granddaughter," he would say to everyone, with his arm resting heavily on her shoulder. "This is *my* little girl."

This possessiveness had filled her thoughts as her father had coaxed and persuaded her to go. "Try it for the rest of the school year, Skeets. If you don't like it out there, you can come home. January to June isn't an eternity."

So she was trying it, trying it with grave misgivings as the jet swept down to its runway.

They met her at the gate. It was her grandmother's voice that attracted her first. "There, that's Karin, that's our girl." She turned and saw her grandmother hurrying toward her, her chubby face beaming. She pulled Karin to her in a hug very much like that her father had given her at the New York airport. Karin felt the warm brush of cheek against hers, the softness of her grandmother's fur collar, smelled the musky scent of violet perfume, and it was almost as if she were a little girl again, being kissed by an adoring grandparent.

"Hello, hello, Kah-rin!" Her grandfather's voice was the same, the same rolling tones with the slight Swedish cadence, and he gave her name the Swedish pronunciation, using a broad *a*. He had both her hands in his, holding her off so he could have a good look at her. "Mamma," he said to her grandmother, "look, she's a real Berglund now. Tall, like the rest of us." His laugh was hearty and pleased. "Why, she's a young lady already!"

"Of course she is, silly," her grandmother said, giving him a nudge. "What did you expect?"

16

Karin was making some notes of her own. Her grandparents' hair had whitened since she last saw them, but otherwise they were much the same, with that Swedish sturdiness. She could not help noticing that even in the crowded air terminal as they got her bags and walked out to the car, people turned to look at her grandfather. He was that kind of man, standing out in a crowd, with his towering height, his shock of almost white hair, and deeply bronzed skin. She was a little surprised, too, at the way he wore his clothes. She had seen him before only in summer slacks and sport shirts, and for some unaccountable reason, she had always pictured him in farmer's garb, but now she saw there was a quiet elegance to his clothes, and he carried them with an air of distinction. So her first surprise was this feeling of pride to be walking with her grandparents, her sweet-faced, still pretty grandmother and the imposing figure of her grandfather.

It was a long ride to Rockridge. Her grandfather drove, talking most of the time, asking Karin questions about her father, about Joan and the new apartment and her father's work.

"You do a little painting yourself, right, Karin?"

"Yes," she answered. "But I only dabble. Dad used to take me on his painting trips. Sometimes I'd smear, sometimes just watch."

"We've got a lot of things besides painting for you to do here." There was laughter in her grandfather's voice. "So it's good you're not head over heels in love with the paintbrushes. Your father was like that, crazy mad for painting pictures." He shook his head. "It is all right in its place, but life's too full of many things. No one should squander himself on just one!"

"Hush, Ed," her grandmother said. "Karin's tired. It's been a long trip for her, and the wedding was a lot of ex-

17

citement too. How was the wedding, dear? "

" The wedding was lovely," she said. " Joan was a beautiful bride. And I was maid of honor. There was a party for them afterward at the apartment of one of their friends. Then they took me right out to the airport."

" It was too bad you had to leave your father so soon after Christmas," her grandmother said in a comforting tone.

" After all those years of your father being alone with you, I was surprised this Joan could catch him so quick," her grandfather commented.

" Hush, Ed," was her grandmother's warning, " they were in love."

Karin was getting the measure of these two, the insistent importance of her grandfather with his strong convictions, and the quiet way her grandmother handled him. Her grandmother clasped her hand during the long ride. I have a friend here, she thought.

Her second surprise came when they swung off the main road and up a long driveway toward a house that rose sharply against the sky line from its cluster of surrounding evergreens. It was a big house, spreading itself to the sides and the back, newly painted a stark white that glistened in the pitch black of winter night. Several evergreens on the long stretch of front lawn were decorated with Christmas lights.

" Why, this looks like an estate! " she stammered her surprise. " I thought you lived on a farm."

Her grandfather's laugh rolled out. " This is a farm. The barns are at the back. Stables too." She saw them in the distance, a group of stone buildings. " If it's farms you're interested in, Karin, you'll see plenty. I have nine others."

Nine others! Her mind raced back in complete confusion, trying to piece together bits of gossip about this energetic

18

grandparent who had been born in Sweden and worked his way up, turning his tremendous vitality and shrewdness to good advantage. She had known he was a farmer but not this kind of farmer. While there had been talk about his extensive investments, no one had mentioned ten farms. Perhaps her father had not really known or had not cared.

If Karin was stunned by the bigness of the house as she stood outside, once inside she felt overwhelmed. The huge living room was rich with deep-piled Oriental rugs in soft Chinese gold, and the floor-length draperies were antique gold satin against which the turquoise and reds of the Victorian chairs glowed brilliantly. There were cranberry and crystal lamps on satinwood tables. Several fine paintings, one of them done by her father, hung on the soft gray walls.

"It's almost too perfect to sit down in!" she exclaimed.

"No, no!" her grandfather laughed, pleased. "We use it all the time. It's a room to live in." He was like a child, enthusiastic, eager to show her everything. "Come, Mamma, we'll show Karin her room."

Her own steps were heavy as she followed his quick ones on the carpeted stairs. Her initial surprise was settling into an alarming worry. How on earth am I ever going to fit into this? she asked herself. Me with my five dresses and two pairs of slacks and handful of sweaters.

Her grandfather's face was alight with pleasure as he threw open one of the doors and, with a sweeping gesture, escorted her in. Her grandmother was close on their heels.

"Karin, here you are. This is your room."

She looked around. It was beautiful.

"Look, we had it done over for you," he said. "Yellow and blue, your favorite colors your father told us. Real Swedish colors." His chuckle was full of delight. "See, the curtains and bedspread and the chairs, everything

19

matches, just the way you like it."

"It's — it's lovely. It really is," she said haltingly, torn between gratitude and the frightening fact that this one room with its dressing nook and bath was larger than the entire first floor of the cottage back in Connecticut.

"Don't you like it?" Her grandfather was looking for more enthusiasm.

"Of course I do," she said quickly. "Anyone would be nuts not to like this, Grandpa." She smiled at her grandmother too. "You've both been swell to me."

Her grandmother patted her arm, seeming to sense her mixed feelings. "You'll feel better after we fill you up with some good hot food."

They had their late supper in the big kitchen and for the first time since her arrival, Karin felt at home. Despite its size, the kitchen was cozy and comfortable. Its only pretensions were to spotless cleanliness and perfect order. So here, amidst the glowing copper and shining chrome, the warm yellow counters and cherry wood paneling, Karin relaxed.

The food was wonderful — *lutfisk*, a special Swedish dish, left over from Christmas; *köttbullar;* herring and potatoes; several kinds of cheese; and for dessert, the traditional rice pudding with one almond.

"There!" her grandfather exclaimed as he made sure that Karin got the almond. "Karin has it, so she'll catch herself a boy friend out here for sure." He laughed. "That is how it works. Whoever gets the almond in the rice pudding will find a husband. Maybe it will be Eric Ringquist. Now there's a fine boy for you, tall, good-looking, steady as a rock!"

Her grandmother, seeing Karin's self-consciousness, changed the subject. "I do my own cooking still," she said, "with only a little help from Mamie." Mamie was a roly-poly little woman who waddled in and out of the

20

kitchen as they ate. She smiled and nodded at Karin, entering into the conversation as if she were one of the family. " Mamie helps with everything," her grandmother explained. " Later she'll go with you to unpack your bags."

Mamie said something in Swedish and both her grandparents laughed. " What did she say? " Karin asked.

" You tell her, Mamma," her grandfather said.

" She says you're one of the prettiest girls she's seen in a long time, tall and fair, with good bones, a real *svenska*, and there will be some broken hearts from now on in Greene County."

Warmed by the food and all this attention, Karin began to expand. She told them about her friends back home and how hard it had been to tear herself away. She talked about the canteen where there had been dances every week and about ski trips up into the mountains and boating and swimming all summer. She even described the little cottage with its homey casualness and its cats and dogs. " A regular army of them under foot all the time," she said, laughing. " Always a new brood of pups and kittens to give away. But I loved it. It almost broke my heart to — " She stopped just in time.

But her grandfather leaned forward, his face serious. " It almost broke your heart to leave. Yah, Karin, we know, we know. But we'll try to fill in the gaps, try to make things up to you and make this a good home for you. We want you to be happy."

She looked away, not wanting to answer even if she had been able to. Her grandfather tried hard to cheer her up. " You will not be lonesome, not for long, with all the young folks here in this town. What about that Mindy Lewis, yah, Mamma, she's a lively little thing, a good one for Karin to meet? " Her grandmother nodded. " And Carla Peterson, now there's a nice girl too. And Eric, that boy I told you about, he will be a good friend, Karin. Our fam-

21

ilies are like this," and her grandfather crossed two of his fingers.

"Hush, Ed," her grandmother said. "Karin is a sensible girl. She will know how to pick her own friends."

Karin folded her napkin and slipped it through the silver napkin ring. "I'd like to meet someone who paints," she said.

Her grandfather almost choked on his last mouthful of rice pudding. His face was scarlet as he exclaimed, "Someone who paints!"

"Yes, paints pictures. Like Dad. Dad had a small class just for fun on Saturdays twice a month. Some awfully nice kids from high school turned out for it. I'd like to meet someone here that's interested in painting."

"There's Steve Fletcher," her grandmother said brightly. "He's the basketball coach's brother, and he paints all the time, every spare minute he can get."

Now it was her grandfather's turn to fold his napkin. He did it carefully, every edge straight, not a crease anywhere, and with every movement, he showed how angry he was.

"Steve Fletcher is nothing for Karin, Mamma. How could you think such a thing?" Her grandfather snorted and Karin almost burst out laughing because he looked so funny when he was really angry, but she managed to hide her amusement.

"A real artist, like your father, that's one thing. Maybe I would have liked him to do something else, but at least he's a success, able to make a living, able to show some pictures in a gallery. But this Steve Fletcher!" He shook his head in disgust. "Your grandmother is right, every spare minute he paints, but such stuff! Great big paintings, full of splashes of color, a lot of paint smeared on any which way."

22

"Oh, you mean he paints modern," Karin said.

"I mean he paints nothing. It says nothing. Nothing to me or to anyone. I think he does not even know what he is doing himself."

"What's he like otherwise?" Karin was interested.

Her grandmother answered. "Tall, dark, thin. A good-looking boy, quiet and well-behaved, Ed, you have to admit, even if he does paint those funny pictures."

"He's not sociable like Eric Ringquist." Her grandfather was adamant. "He takes walks by himself. When he isn't painting, his nose is in a book."

"Is that such a crime? To take walks and read books and be quiet?" her grandmother demanded.

Her grandfather whacked the table with the palm of his hand. "I do not think Steve Fletcher is good for Karin," he said. "He has moods. I do not like moods in a boy."

Karin was tired, very tired, from the trip and the excitement of the wedding before that, or she might not have answered so bluntly. Now her grandparents' arguments, tossed back and forth over her head, rubbed her already raw nerves.

"Grandpa," she said quietly, "I think Grandma's right. I ought to be allowed to pick my friends for myself without help from anyone. I'll decide for myself whether or not to like Steve."

He stared her full in the face, shocked for once into silence. His face burned a deep scarlet, and she could see him grappling with his temper. Then he burst out laughing. Loud laughter shook his huge frame and echoed and re-echoed in the big kitchen.

"Yah, Mamma," he said, "she is her father's daughter. This girl of ours has a mind of her own. She speaks up to me."

Her grandmother did not answer, but Mamie, busy at

23

the sink, said something in Swedish. Karin's grandmother gave a sharp command, also in Swedish, and Mamie, mumbling to herself, left the room.

"What did she say?" Karin asked.

"Never mind, dear," her grandmother said. "I think it would be good if we turned in early tonight. It's been a big day for all of us."

Later when Karin was alone in her room with Mamie, putting her few belongings in the vast empty closet and bureau drawers, she asked Mamie what she had said in Swedish.

Mamie enjoyed a quiet laugh before she answered. "I said you are not so much your father's daughter as your grandfather's. Full of spunk, to answer him like that about picking your own friends." Her laugh trailed off into a chuckle. "I said you are cut from the same stick of dynamite, you two, the old one and the young one. I think some time the two sticks rub each other the wrong way, and we hear a pretty good explosion in Greene County."

CHAPTER | 2

THE FIRST big "explosion" came at dinner on Karin's second night in her grandparents' home.

It was a hectic day, full of excitement, with never a moment for homesickness. In the morning her grandfather appeared at the kitchen door while Karin was having a breakfast of Swedish pancakes with lingonberries and tiny homemade sausages.

"Bundle up good, Karin. We're taking a long ride."

This time he did not do the driving. Karin was sandwiched in the front seat of the station wagon between her

24

grandfather and the driver, a lanky man with thick black hair and a youthful grin that showed strong white teeth. In contrast to these signs of youth, the man's face was crisscrossed with a network of fine lines, and his skin had the leathery look of age.

"This is Oscar," her grandfather said. "I knew him in Sweden."

She felt the sudden response to Oscar that one does, at first meeting, to people who are destined to become fast friends.

"Pleased to meet you, Karin." He gave her name the Swedish pronunciation. "Mamie told me you favored the Berglunds in looks."

"Yah, that's right," her grandfather nodded his pleasure, adding: "Mamie is Oscar's wife. Together they take care of your grandmother and me. Mamie watches over the house, Oscar over the barns and stables. They are our friends."

Karin got her grandfather's message that Oscar was to be treated as Mamie had been last night, as one of the family.

That morning, they made the circuit of the farms. Karin learned something of what it meant to be a Berglund in Greene County. Now she realized what her father had meant when he had said, "Your grandfather's a big wheel out there, Karin." Every time her grandfather hopped out of the car and strode toward a group of workmen, there was the hearty: "Good morning, Mr. Berglund. We've got those reports ready for you. Hope everything suits you. Fine winter day, Mr. Berglund."

Karin came in for her share of attention. Almost invariably the greeting from farm superintendents and foremen was: "So, this is Ed Berglund's granddaughter. We've heard a lot about you. Hope you'll like it here."

The overseer of one farm was more loquacious. "Yes, ma'am, I remember when your grandfather came down from Minnesota and bought his first farm in Greene County. He was just past eighteen and spoke every third word in Swedish. But he was smart and shrewd even as a boy. Wanted me to put up some money with him when he spread out. I was cautious and didn't. You see what happened. Your granddad's my boss, and I'm working for him! " There was more admiration than envy in the voice. " You can be proud to be Ed Berglund's granddaughter."

This was to be the catchword of the morning, Ed Berglund's granddaughter. When she was alone with Oscar while her grandfather discussed some private matter with one of the men, she said half-humorously: " I guess there's a label pinned on me already. Ed Berglund's granddaughter. Makes me feel almost like a piece of property."

She had meant the words to be witty, but they tumbled out sharp, almost cutting. Oscar looked at her quietly before he answered.

" Even for a joke, I think you will be careful not to say anything like this to your grandfather, yah, Karin? He is a proud man and of nothing more proud this moment than that he has a fine tall *svenska* of a granddaughter. You will be careful not to hurt him, yah? "

" Yah," she said, grinning. " I'll be careful."

She remembered Oscar's warning all that afternoon, although it was certainly not the easiest bit of advice to follow. At lunch, which Karin tackled with great gusto after her morning ride of the circuit, her grandfather announced that they were going to Grandville. " To buy some clothes," he said.

" But I have clothes," she answered.

He laughed as he took his second helping of noodles and meat. " So we will buy you some more. They have good

26

stores in Grandville. Styles from New York and some from Paris too."

Again she was bundled into a car, this time one of the sedans, and whisked off with her grandparents on a shopping tour.

Her grandfather bought with a lavish hand that first amazed, then startled her. Everything she tried on, that was becoming and fit well, he wanted to buy for her. In less time than most people would take to select one good dress, he had bought her a navy broadcloth suit and a heathery tweed, a half dozen school dresses in the finest woolens Karin had ever touched, four skirts with cashmere sweaters to match, shoes, handbags, gloves, stockings.

"Now," he said, his cheeks flushed, his eyes sparkling, "now we'll go to the French room at Brunberg's."

Karin protested, but her grandmother put her arm around her. "Karin, we love you very much and it's a long time since we've had someone young to fuss over. Let your grandfather have his way, just this once."

So she did, but with reluctance, and with a feeling of guilt and a touch of hurt pride. She did not want to accept so much. It was enough to be living with them, to have them do over a room for her and go to all the trouble they already had. But she saw that a refusal would hurt them more than an acceptance, so she tagged along.

In the French room, he bought her clothes, "for best" as her grandmother called them. The first price tag she glanced at shocked Karin so much that she dared not even look at another.

She was giddy, heady with the excitement of this strange, wonderful, exasperating Cinderella day. There were times when she felt that it was happening to someone else, not to her, and that almost any moment she would wake up and find that it had all been a fantastic dream.

At last she tried on fur coats, the first she had ever slipped into except last Christmas when Bet Stevens was given a mouton and let Karin try it on.

These were no moutons! Here Karin felt her will power slipping, feeling the magnetic attraction of the costly and the beautiful and the suddenly available. "I've always wanted a fur coat of my own," she said wistfully.

"And you shall have it!" There was jubilance in her grandfather's voice as she selected a sheared beaver, the finest the store had to offer.

Her pulse quickened as she slipped into it. She walked around the mirrored room catching glimpses of herself. It's beautiful, she thought, the loveliest thing I've ever owned.

She squelched her pride, in the thrill of owning this handsome coat. Then, as the head of the department stood by, smiling at Karin and holding her grandfather's check in her hands, she said a disturbing thing to Karin.

"You look charming in it, Miss Berglund. You're fortunate to be the granddaughter of Mr. Berglund."

It was that afternoon that she met Eric Ringquist. It seemed to come about in the most casual way, yet Karin could sense that it was as planned as the trip to the French Room at Brunberg's.

On the way home, her grandfather swung off the road at the farm just before his own.

"I have business with Ingmar Ringquist," he said. "Mamma, you and Karin better come in with me. It's cold out here, and I'll be quite a little while."

Eric came into the kitchen at a booming summons from her grandfather, who stood at the foot of the stairs and shouted, "Eric, come down, I have someone here for you to meet."

There was the clatter of boy's shoes, then a tall blond

boy burst into the room. Karin liked him at once, liked his good-natured grin, his straight posture, the honest way he looked at her from eyes as blue as the calico curtains at the windows.

Real Swedish blue, she thought with amusement. A true *svensk*, as the old-timers would say. I'm learning the lingo!

"Karin," her grandfather said, "this is Eric, son of my best friend. Eric, my granddaughter from Connecticut. You two have plenty in common, yah. You both like good times and sports."

Karin was left alone with Eric by obvious design, in that wonderfully good-smelling Swedish kitchen, with its aroma of applesauce cake and saffron bread freshly baked.

The grin never faded from Eric's face, but Karin did not take this attempt at matchmaking so cheerfully. Embarrassment confused her, shaking her poise. She was accustomed to picking her friends, whether boys or girls, and she did not like the uncomfortable feeling of being thrown at Eric.

"I bet you don't like this any more than I do," she said with her usual bluntness.

"I don't mind it at all," he said with a humorous twinkle and an engaging drawl. "In fact, I almost like it." She looked sharply into his amused eyes.

"But it all seems so — so planned. I should think you'd hate having a girl thrown at you like this." She forced a smile. "It's so terribly old-fashioned."

"Yes, it is, I guess. We're supposed to like each other very much. Sort of a tradition. Families that were best friends over there," he nodded as if Sweden were down the road, "try to steer their young folks toward one another. Don't let it throw you, Karin. We're not going to be any better friends than you want us to be. Although this time an old Swedish tradition has given me a break."

29

"Thanks, Eric," she said, grateful for his understanding.

"How about it if I call you 'Skeets'?"

"Why, that's my father's pet name for me! How'd you know about it?"

"Your grandmother told Mamie and Mamie told Oscar and Oscar told me."

"I can see this is going to be an awfully small town," she said, smiling.

"Wait till you join the girls basketball team, Skeets. Now there's a cozy little gossip circle for you. You'll have no secrets."

"But I haven't even thought of joining up for basketball. The season's on already, and I'll have enough to think about with a new school and all."

"You'll join up, Skeets."

"How can you be so sure?"

"Well, anyone who's anybody in Greene County plays basketball, unless you've got a broken leg or have to wear bifocals." He laughed. "And besides, your granddad may accept the fact that the boy on the next farm isn't your dream man. But he'll never let you off from girls basketball."

So she was ready for it when her grandfather introduced the subject at dinner that night.

During the soup course her grandfather looked up and said, "Of course you play basketball, Karin."

"I played a pretty good game of guard on the varsity back home."

"Good. You'll play guard here then."

"But can they put me on the team just like that?" she asked, snapping her fingers. "I should think they'd have to try me out. Besides, basketball's pretty big stuff out here. You Midwesterners go all out for it. Personally, I happen to like skiing better. Maybe we could find a nice big hill for me to schuss down while we leave the basketball to the really top-notch experts." She tried to make light of it. Actually she felt she was going to have enough adjustments to make during this winter without trying to compete in Midwestern basketball.

Her grandfather stiffened. "Karin, I think you are making a joke of basketball. I happen to be chairman of the recreation committee, and basketball is not a joking matter to me."

"I wasn't being funny, Gramp. I was dead serious."

"No matter, we won't argue about it. I'm glad you play the game. Tomorrow we'll run over to school and watch the team practice. They have been practicing all Christmas vacation. You can meet the girls and Miss Fletcher, the coach."

So the next afternoon her grandfather drove her over to Rockridge High School. There, in a gymnasium bigger than the school itself, she was given her first taste of Midwestern girls basketball.

Individually, the playing was terrific. Even in this practice game, the girls, each of them, played the kind of taut, controlled game played by star players in the white heat of interschool competition back home. Their passing, feinting, pivoting were exceptional. Every forward appeared an expert at some kind of shot. It was clear they took their basketball as seriously as Karin's grandfather did!

Yet something was lacking.

She could not, during this first quick appraisal, tell exactly what was wrong. Something was fouled up, she was sure. While the individual playing was tops, there seemed to be some lack of team co-ordination. Once or twice Karin sat forward, her shoulders hunched, her hands clenched, as she wished she could get out there into the huddle of guards, slap the ball from their hands, and heave it across the court to the waiting forwards.

"Come on," her grandfather tugged at her coat sleeve. "Practice is almost over. I'll introduce you."

So Karin met Miss Fletcher, a tall, dark woman with a quiet voice and manner. Then, in a dizzy whirl of names, she was introduced to the girls on the team.

Miss Fletcher chatted a few moments with Karin.

"I understand you're coming out for the team."

"My grandfather wants me to."

"Don't *you* want to, Karin?"

"Well, sure, I guess so." She warmed to Miss Fletcher's friendly manner. She grinned. "Since there aren't any hills to ski on and I like sports, I guess I'll have to settle for this. The girls play a swell game. I mean, individually. They're tops." She noticed a faint flush creep up from Miss Fletcher's throat.

"'Individually, they're tops,'" she repeated Karin's words. "That means you noticed a lack of team spirit."

"Oh, I wouldn't say that!" Karin said quickly.

"Then let me say it. There *is* a lack of team spirit. And if you're going to be one of us you might as well know about it. These girls had a man coach before I came here. His name was Bo Jensen and he liked a rough, tough game. Then your grandfather imported me from the East and I changed everything, upsetting the applecart."

"Are you from the East too?" Karin asked, surprised.

"Yes, can't you tell from all those terrible broad *a*'s?" Karin joined in her laugh.

Good, Karin thought. She's got a sense of humor, even about herself.

Miss Fletcher walked down the gym with Karin while her grandfather stood talking with a group of the girls. "We haven't had too good a season, Karin. Last year we trailed at the tail end of the county tournament. This year we're off to another slow start. If you can play the game well, you ought to consider joining in with us. We could use some new blood."

"I guess I'm feeling a little timid about it. You know, I've always been in awe of the way Midwestern girls play basketball. Their speed is terrific, their shooting is tops."

"Don't be overawed." The coach was smiling in that friendly way. "If a girl is good in sports, she's good in sports, no matter what part of the country she comes from."

"That gives me some encouragement," Karin said. "I'm glad you feel that way."

"I do feel that way." The coach held out her hand and Karin shook it warmly.

"I think it would break my grandfather's heart if I didn't try out for this team."

"I think it would," Miss Fletcher answered with an emphatic nod.

She left Karin to have a few words with her grandfather. A bright-eyed girl with an inquisitive expression left the group of girls and came over to Karin.

"You lost my name in the shuffle, I'll bet," she said pleasantly. "I'm Mindy Lewis."

"Oh, yes, I've heard about you."

"Already?" Mindy laughed. She counted off on her fingers. "One, I'm a busybody. Two, I talk too much. Three, I'm the shortest girl on the team, a mere five foot six among those amazons. Four, I'm crazy about Eric Ringquist, but he can't see me for sour apples."

"Wrong on all four counts. Gramp said you'd be fun to know."

"Well, good for Gramp!" She grinned. "I think you'll be fun too. How do you like our team?"

33

"You'd play a terrific game — if you could only get together."

"You noticed that too?" Karin nodded. "Miss Fletcher's got a problem. Some of the girls don't like her."

"Why not? I do. She seems friendly and sociable. Not a bit bossy, and yet she knows her stuff. I thought she coached very well," Karin said. "She looked good from where I was sitting."

"Most teams around here have men coaches, Karin. We had one too before Miss Fletcher. A regular whiz of a guy. We played for blood then. A rough, fast, terrific game. You have to play like that if you want to survive with some of the teams in Greene County."

"You mean the girls liked Bo Jensen and so they decided not to like Miss Fletcher. As a result, they're off their game."

"It's not as simple as that." Mindy shook her head. "Miss Fletcher has a lot of theories, and some of the girls don't think they work out in practice. She's a stickler for the rule book, coaches a very ladylike game of basketball. She believes that girls can play a good solid game and still remain ladies. Your grandfather is all for that. In fact, he's practically crammed Miss Fletcher and her theories down the whole town's throat. I think that's our biggest problem. Everybody's confused and sort of upset."

"I know. Gramp can do that sort of thing."

"You've been here two days, and you've already discovered that?" The two girls looked at each other with humor in their eyes.

Karin winked at Mindy. "I've been here two days, and I've had a few things crammed down my throat too! Including, if I may be so bold as to say so, Midwestern basketball!"

CHAPTER | 3

U. S.1281546

KARIN ENROLLED at Rockridge High School the next week. She liked the smallness of the place. It was intimate and pleasant, especially after the sprawling campus high school she had attended in Connecticut. Within a few days she felt remarkably at ease in her classrooms. There was little difference between the subject matter and curriculum of the two schools despite their contrast in size.

Most of her teachers were young. Mrs. Francis, history, had a sense of humor. Mr. Drake, math, was deliberate, droll, and seemed to understand that girls often found his subject difficult. Mr. Somers, science, was enthusiastic, the kind of personality that brought students flocking around him. Miss Matthews, English, was precise, a bit old-maidish with her prim clothes and meticulous instructions that had to be followed to the letter — or else! But she liked young people and understood them, so Karin soon grew fonder of Miss Matthews than of any of her other teachers.

For several days she went dizzily through the whirl of adjustment. It was exciting to be a new girl. She got lots of attention. Some of the girls admired her new clothes. Others were more interested in her as a person. Some wanted to know what was it like to live on the East Coast, so near the ocean, so near New York. New York seemed a mecca to them, the place they dreamed of going to someday.

" It's big and noisy and crowded," she told them. " I was always sort of glad to get back to Connecticut."

The boys were attentive too, flattering Karin with compliments and playful teasing. In those first days at Rockridge High, Eric was almost always at Karin's side, taking her under his wing and making her his personal responsibility. They were both juniors, so they had several classes together. It was Eric who saw that she found the right classrooms, who introduced her to teachers and other students.

In classes she often let her glance stray toward where Eric sat — invariably in a seat near the window — and whenever she looked at him, she discovered he was staring at her. Sometimes she would turn quickly away because Eric's face was an open one, completely honest, and she thought she knew what it was saying to her.

You're what I've been waiting for a long, long time, he seemed to be telling her.

It was Eric who, oddly enough, introduced her to Steve Fletcher. Ever since the night of her arrival when her grandparents had argued over her head about Steve, Karin had her ears pricked up for information about him.

The more she heard about Steve, the more fascinated she became. There were two schools of thought, both among the girls and the boys, so the reports were conflicting, and they baffled Karin. Steve was "brilliant" or he was a "dud," an "egghead drip." He could be the life of the party once you got him out, and he warmed up. He played the hottest jazz piano in Rockridge. But he was also considered withdrawn, "unsociable," and very choosy about the people he wanted as friends. He was devoted to his sister, defended her to the hilt against criticism around the school and the town, yet he shunned girls basketball as if it were the plague.

He liked girls and girls liked him — how could they help it, Karin heard them say, when Steve was so attractive? Yet there seemed to be a reputation for fickleness. Or was it just that Steve lost interest quickly because the girls he was drawn to were shallow or had difficult personalities? Take Liz Ekstrom, for example. Liz was a guard on the basketball team, but she was a real " goon." Steve had taken her out a few times, then dropped her like a hot cake when she started the clinging vine act around the school. It was rumored that Steve had summed Liz up in one clean-cut sentence, " I don't like sentimental slosh."

Well, neither did Karin, but if Steve had really said that in public about Liz, it did seem a little cruel.

Yet Karin was enormously curious about Steve. She pumped for information with what tact she could summon. The more she heard, the more unpredictable and complex he became.

About his paintings there was practically no disagreement. Most of the kids seemed to share her grandfather's sentiments. " You should see that stuff. What a waste of canvas and paint! Huge canvases splotched with color — crazy reds and greens and blues and purples and oranges. Wow, how that guy loves orange! And you can't make out a single thing. Just a hodgepodge of lines and circles. Looks like the colored illustration for a geometry book. That guy *thinks* he can paint." A derisive laugh. " Not for my money! "

Karin was not so sure. Her father was an academic painter for the most part, painting in the " traditional " way with only an occasional splurge — for fun — into abstract expressionism. Yet Karin had been taken to The Museum of Modern Art and The Whitney Museum of American Art, and she had been taught by her father to appreciate something of what this ultramodern school was trying to say.

So she wanted very much to know Steve Fletcher. For a while it seemed as if her wish would never be granted because Steve appeared as illusive as his character seemed

contradictory. He was a senior, so they had no classes together. In the halls, she caught a few fleeting glimpses of
him, and she liked what she saw. Yet he never seemed
to know that she existed — and in this respect he was
very different from the boys who flocked around the " new
girl."

Then, one day as she and Eric were sauntering out of
Miss Matthews' English class together, their heads close
as Eric asked Karin's advice about a theme he was doing,
she almost bumped into Steve Fletcher. She caught herself in time, and he drew back and apologized, although it
had really been her fault. For a moment they stood staring
into each other's faces. Her stare was frankly curious and
his was the owlish, serious stare of the person who wants
to paint everything he looks at.

" Karin," Eric said, " I'd like you to meet Steve Fletcher.
You two should have a lot in common, Steve. Karin's father
is a successful artist."

" Yes, so I've heard," Steve said. His smile was faint.
Well, he's truthful, anyway, Karin thought. He admits he's
heard of me even though he's acted as if I didn't exist.
Then he said something that made her pulse beat hard and
her spirits soar. " I've been waiting until the new-girl-in-
town furor calmed down a little, Karin. Then I thought we
could have a hamburger together and get to know each
other."

" I'd love it," she said, too quickly.

He seemed in no hurry to move on, chatting in the hall
with her. He had a studio he said, in the barn on the place
he and his sister rented. Downstairs she had a basketball
court and small gym rigged up. Upstairs he painted to his
heart's content. Karin would have to come over and see it.

The buzzer told them they were late for their next class.
Eric tugged at the sleeve of Karin's sweater. She turned,

having almost forgotten he was there. She hurried down the hall with Eric by her side, not seeing him, not hearing what he was saying, not even caring that they were late for class.

So she had met Steve Fletcher at last, and she could see that he was everything people said he was, everything and more. He was surely difficult, surely hard to know and understand. But he was stimulating and mature for his age. He had all the things Karin admired in a boy, poise, intelligence, depth, and even a sly wit. New-girl-in-town furor indeed!

"Hey, you." It was Eric's voice calling her back. "You with the stars in your eyes." She looked at Eric and flushed self-consciously. "Never mind, Skeets," he whispered as he opened the door to Mr. Somers' classroom, "I don't mind a little competition." He was grinning at her. "Besides, I knew my luck with the old Swedish tradition wouldn't last forever."

That afternoon she made the basketball team. It was not even a tryout in the most elementary meaning of that term. She walked into the gym, and Miss Fletcher handed her a Rockridge uniform and told her she was on the third string, substitute guard. She joined the third string cooling its heels on the benches while they watched the varsity and second string play a practice game.

Her thoughts were disturbed. Something seemed wrong. Miss Fletcher had spoken to her in such a friendly way on the day of their first meeting, had even asked her to join the team. Now she was being treated in this strange way. Had Miss Fletcher merely been nice that day because Karin was Ed Berglund's granddaughter, and he had hired the coach? Or was she being careful not to show Karin too much attention today for that very reason. Karin sat there, feeling out of things, unhappy and quite unwanted for the

39

first time since she had hit this warmhearted Midwestern town.

There wasn't anyone she could talk to about it. Mindy, whom she had got to know better in classes, was out there on the court. Good old Eric wasn't around to take her hand and comfort her. This afternoon she was completely on her own.

She sat and sat and sat. If this is the way it's going to be, she thought, I guess I won't show up tomorrow. But she thought it over that night. Basketball wasn't her first love, she told herself, so what difference did it make if her little old ego got rubbed the wrong way this once? She had gone into this sport mostly to please her grandfather. Not just in submission to his strong will. She had proved that her own was a match for his! However, her grandparents were doing all they could to make her happy, and she felt that the least she could do was try to please them in return.

Yet, strangely enough, the minute she had signed up for basketball, her feelings about it had changed. Reluctant to enter, once in, she wanted to make the grade.

I'll go back tomorrow, she told herself before she fell asleep, and see what happens.

On the second day of practice, Miss Fletcher put her into the game at once, playing guard against the varsity forwards. Karin was so surprised to find herself in action on the court that she forgot to be self-conscious. She played hard, the best game she could. Against Mindy Lewis, Carla Peterson, and Babs Fairchild, the varsity forwards, she made a poor showing. She could not stop their flow of shots. The other guards shouted instructions, commands, and criticisms to her. This made her angry and she took on a new spurt of energy. She played hard-hitting basketball, full steam ahead, until she thought she would drop. Miss

Fletcher took her out just in time.

Before the second game began, Miss Fletcher said, "Karin, you go in and warm up with the forwards."

"But I can't shoot."

"Do as I ask, please."

Bewildered, Karin took her place in the string of forwards lined up for shooting drill.

She was terrified. When her turn came, the ball was hurled toward her. It stung her hands. She smelled the leather, felt the impact. Her grip was taut and awkward. With a clumsy twist of the wrists she tossed blindly at the target. The ball teetered on the rim, toppled off.

There was no time to think. The line moved fast as the girls passed, caught the ball, pivoted, and shot. Karin's turn came all too soon. Again the ball stung her hands, again she clutched it with a hard grip.

"Loosen up, Karin." It was Mindy's voice. "Hold it that split second before you shoot. Take aim and then fire!"

She listened and obeyed. She paused, aimed, hefted the ball in a chest shot. It teetered, but this one went in.

"Nice going!" Mindy called.

More shocked than pleased, Karin ran to take her place for the next try. A lucky fluke, she told herself. Yet she knew it hadn't been quite that. Mindy's advice had helped.

She made a third basket and a fourth. It was fun! She was enjoying herself. Lots of times she missed, but often she made it too. Out of the twenty-five shots she tried she made a clean-cut eleven.

Dazed, she almost staggered across the floor toward the benches. After practice, Miss Fletcher detained her.

"Karin, I'd like you to drop over this evening to my place for a little while. I want to test you out with some special shots on the basketball court in our barn."

41

It was on the tip of Karin's tongue to ask questions: What for? What's this all about? What's the big idea of making me go through test shots? Why all this crazy business of putting me in the string of forwards this afternoon?

These and a half dozen other questions were squelched into silence. There was no use in trying to figure out this basketball coach with her unorthodox methods.

What a character! she thought. Even if she is from the same part of the country as I am, and we ought to stick together out here in this land of the wide-open spaces — she's still a character!

Then her doubts and questions were silenced by a new thought. It was the barn Miss Fletcher was inviting her to, and over the barn was the place where that attractive brother of hers painted what everyone called his crazy, meaningless pictures!

CHAPTER | 4

KARIN SWUNG her grandfather's sedan into the parking place outside the Fletcher barn. She liked the way the car handled. It seemed good to be driving a car like this after the jalopies she and her father had run around in. Her new license had been granted this afternoon. Even so, her grandfather had wanted Oscar to come over with her this evening, but she had talked him out of it.

"If I'm safe on the hills of New England, I'm doubly safe on the flat prairies," she had answered. Ozzie, darling that he was, would have cramped her style.

She glanced up at the top story of the barn — the former hayloft, she supposed. It was brightly lighted with the daylight lamps used by painters for night work, and she could make out a tall figure moving back and forth.

"I wonder if I'll really get to see him," she muttered as she climbed out and strode toward the barn door.

Miss Fletcher came to the door in answer to the pounding of the old iron knocker.

"Hi, Karin," she said. "Come on in. I've been waiting for you. Glad you could make it so early."

Outside, the old barn had looked a bit gloomy with its peeling gray paint, its barren surroundings without trees or bushes. Inside, however, the picture changed, for there was a cheerful atmosphere in the small gymnasium into which Karin followed the coach. The floor was marked off as a basketball court, with its lines and circles. Several baskets hung from their backboards. There were chin bars and mattresses tossed around the edge of the court and not so long ago someone had given a party here, for the decorations were still up.

"This looks like fun," Karin said.

"We've enjoyed it," Miss Fletcher answered. She took Karin's coat and scarf and tossed them onto a chair. Then suddenly she was all business.

"I hope I didn't frighten you when I said I wanted to give you some tests."

"Not in the least, but I'll admit my curiosity is sizzling."

"Good. We'll satisfy that at once. I understand you passed your driving test today. In some ways this won't be too much different."

"They said my eyesight was perfect," Karin said. "'Almost phenomenal' were the officer's words."

Miss Fletcher nodded. "I thought as much," she said. "Now, let's go." She stood Karin behind a line and told her to bounce the ball at a certain mark on the wall. She had to bounce *at* the mark, then above, below, to the right, to the left.

43

When Miss Fletcher was satisfied with whatever information this gave her, she brought out the equipment for visual tests.

"They're called depth perception and peripheral vision tests," she explained. "I'm trying to find out how good your side vision is. How well you can judge distances to a basket and the speed of the ball."

Miss Fletcher then took her on the basketball court. She tossed Karin the ball from various spots, calling out at what point she wanted Karin to shoot.

"I'm not good at this," Karin protested. "I've always played guard position."

"You shot well this afternoon," Miss Fletcher insisted. "Give it another try."

So Karin followed orders. She caught the passes and hurled them at the basket. She knew that her footwork was clumsy, her shots far from scientific. She had all she could do to catch the ball as it zoomed at her from Miss Fletcher's hard passes and hurtle it through space at the basket. She was still a little surprised whenever she saw it go through the net.

Nearly exhausted, she threw herself down on one of the mattresses. Miss Fletcher sat on a bench nearby. She was silent, watching Karin lie there, face down, her shoulders heaving from the strenuous exercise.

When she spoke her manner was deliberate, her voice soothing. "Karin, what I'm going to say is bound to surprise you." She waited until Karin twisted around. "You should never have played guard position in basketball. I believe you're a natural forward."

Karin digested the words slowly. Many things crowded her mind, comments she had heard the girls make about Miss Fletcher, some of them humorous but often sarcastic. "We're playing the game *scientifically*," they would gibe.

"We're crammed full of psychology. Now who ever heard of an intellectual approach to basketball?" A sneer followed this. "We're the joke of the whole county. Know what they call us? 'Slide-rule Fletcher's Scientific Marvels.'"

Yet Karin was won over by Miss Fletcher, as she had been from the first moment she laid eyes on this woman. She liked the coach's attitude and manner. She was not trying to bully Karin into playing forward. She wasn't even acting high hat about it, as if she had made some tremendous discovery. And there wasn't a speck of domination in her approach. She wasn't saying: Look, you've got the makings of a good forward and by hook or by crook I'm going to make you one! Nothing like that.

It was more a kind of persuasiveness. It was as if she were trying to win Karin over to doing what was best for her and the team.

Karin took a long look at Miss Fletcher, waiting with some eagerness for her reply.

She resembled Steve. You could see the family likeness, handsome head with wiry, dark hair, deep-set eyes that bored through whatever they looked at, the chiseled, tapering nose. Only the mouths were different. Steve's was sensitive. His sister's was firm and strong.

Karin could see that the decision was to be her own.

"What would I have to do?" she asked.

Miss Fletcher's eyes sparked with interest. "You'd have to work hard, very hard. I'd give you all the help and time I could. You'd have to put in a lot of time too and willingness. Most important of all would be willingness."

Karin thought it over. A few days ago she would have bowed out as gracefully as possible. But that was then. Things had happened in these last few days. For one thing, she felt drawn by now into the closeness of Rockridge High

45

School. There was a spirit to this place, the spirit and warmth and closeness of a small school with small classes where everyone knew everyone. Already she felt part of this, felt she belonged.

But more than this had happened. There had been an undeniable thrill this afternoon in heaving those balls at that metal rim. It had proved far more exciting than jumping to intercept a pass from forward to forward. It had been an electric something, a real kick every time that ball plopped through the net.

"I'm willing," she said to Miss Fletcher.

"Good," Miss Fletcher said. "I'm glad, Karin. I can use another good forward on that team and with your vision, your eye for the basket, I think you'll make very rapid progress. Now perhaps you'd like to see Steve's studio. He'd like you to go on up. I have some reports I must work on down here."

Steve's voice was welcoming at the top of the stairs.

"Come on up and have a look around," he called.

She sauntered around his studio, trying to concentrate on what she saw, when she was so much more interested in Steve himself than in his paintings. She could see now what the kids at school and her grandfather had been getting at. Steve's stuff was so modern that the average layman would think it was hideous. But she, an artist's daughter, could see beyond the still amateurish brushwork to a strong vein of talent. She had been exposed to enough painting to realize that this stuff was original, personal, and promising. Furthermore, despite the school crowd's snide remarks about the colors, Steve did have a gift in that direction.

"Can you stand it?" he asked, and in that moment of modesty she saw a side of Steve that she realized was carefully hidden behind a front of bravado.

46

"Stand it? Don't talk like that," she said. "You have a great deal of talent, Steve."

"Coming from you I appreciate that," he said slowly. "I don't get much praise, you know. No one around here understands this stuff. They think it's awful. They say I can't draw, that's why I paint like this." He grabbed some sketches from a portfolio on a shelf and shoved them toward her. "But I can draw. See, look at these."

"Of course you can draw. I can tell by looking at your canvases."

"Can you? Can you honestly?" He almost shoved her into a chair in his eagerness. "Sit down. Let's talk. Let's talk about everything, about painting and you and me and well, just everything."

She could feel the hunger in his voice, hunger for companionship and understanding. And she knew too that he must have got precious little of it from the crowd at school. It wasn't that they would set out deliberately to be mean. It was just that they could not reach him any more than he could reach them. She saw and she understood.

So Steve poured himself out to her sympathetic ears. He showed her everything he had painted, all the early paintings as well as the new ones. He told her how his sister had done so much for him, encouraging him, managing always to see that he had someplace to paint, even a tiny corner of the living room when they had lived in an apartment back east.

At last he stopped, seeming to pause for breath as much as anything. "Well! I've sure rattled on, Karin. This is awful, talking so much about myself. You haven't had a chance."

"I don't mind. I like to listen to you." She was telling the truth. "This fills a kind of gap for me too, Steve. Being around paints, canvases, the smell of turpentine and lin-

47

seed oil." She got up and threw out her arms. "It's wonderful to stand here in the middle of all this sloppy mess again!"

He laughed, and she laughed with him. "So we were both a little homesick for something, right?" he asked.

"Right."

"Let me make you some coffee."

"Can you? Here?"

"Sure. I've got everything, including the kitchen sink."

So they had coffee and homemade cake, which his sister had donated, and they sat until Karin jumped up and said: "Oh, my goodness, my grandfather will disown me! I've stayed a half hour overtime, and my homework's not done. Oh, my goodness!"

Steve looked at her quizzically. "You're cute," he said. "I like the way you said that 'oh, my goodness!' As if you were a freckled-faced kid about ten with pigtails." He studied her face. "Sometime I'd like to do a portrait of you, Karin."

"As a freckled-faced kid with pigtails?"

He laughed, shaking his head.

"You do portraits too?"

"Not many. I'm working on a few now. But you can't see them," he added quickly, "not until they're finished."

"Good, that will give me an excuse to come back sometime."

Downstairs Karin said good night to Miss Fletcher, and Steve walked out to the car with her.

"You don't ever need an excuse to come back here, Karin. The latchkey is always out." He paused, then added: "This has been one of the most exciting and wonderful evenings of my life, Karin. You don't know how much you've done for me. Thanks. Thanks a million."

"Thanks too," she said. "In fact, thanks two million."

48

He leaned down and kissed her, lightly on the cheek. " I loved every minute of it," he said. Then he kissed her on the other cheek. She drove off, gripping the wheel hard, feeling the friction on her moist palms, and feeling a warm flush in her cheeks.

CHAPTER | 5

So KARIN was caught up in the life of Rockridge. The big house still overwhelmed her, but there were things even about this that she was growing to like. Beneath the steady bustle of farm management lay a quiet way of life, which Karin discovered was gracious and relaxed.

That life centered around her grandmother's kitchen, the small dining room in which they had their pleasant meals, and the family sitting room. Her life was not the same as it had been back in Connecticut. She did not enjoy the closeness with her grandparents that she had had with her father, but there were compensations.

She had her pick of the horses, and this pleased her far more than the closetful of new clothes. Oscar was teaching her to ride " western." Afternoons and weekends when she wasn't busy with basketball or homework, she often rode out with Oscar. She enjoyed his wry philosophy and humor.

He was intensely interested in all her school activities, especially basketball. " How're you getting along with heaving that piece of blown-up leather into the old peach basket? " he asked.

" I wish I knew! I go over to Miss Fletcher's barn after basketball practice every day. She works me like a dog, tossing shots, passing, feinting. My arms get so tired I think they'll fall off. Then, back on the basketball court at school, she lets me sit on the bench. I can't figure why."

"Some good reason, for sure. That is a smart woman, Karin. You must not sell her short."

"I'm not. I know she's smart. She makes a lot more sense than her brother, in lots of ways."

"How is that?"

"Ozzie, let me ask you this. How would you figure a boy who makes a big fuss over you when you go to his studio, likes your company, talks your ear off, even shows he's fond of you? Then in school where most boys chase after the girls they like, he lets me alone. Sometimes he even acts as if we were strangers." She was getting something out of her system. "I like to get a note once in a while from a boy. I like him to ask me to go to a movie or something. Now I ask you, how do you figure him?"

"Karin, a long time ago I learned not to try to figure too close the people I like. Just to let them alone, let them be themselves."

"Oh, come on, Ozzie. Open up a little. You've known Steve a lot longer than I have. What do you think of him?"

"Sure I know him. He comes over on errands once in a while. I see him around town, at church suppers with his sister. And I see him take long walks alone. Sometimes with his paintbox. You know, once he asked me to pose for a picture."

"No kidding, Ozzie!"

"Yah, no kidding. I stop to give him a lift and he say: 'Oscar, I like your face. It is strong and has a lot of character. Look, let me make a sketch of you, yah?' So I say yah." Oscar's chest swelled. It was plain that he was very proud to have a face full of strength and character, a face Steve would want to sketch.

"Now tell me, Ozzie, what do you think of Steve? Do

50

you like him? Like him a lot, I mean?"

"I think the question better be, do *you* like him a lot, Karin?"

She glanced away, flushing.

"So that is the way it is. Then I tell you it is no good for me to say whether I like Steve. A girl in love, she makes up her own mind."

"I didn't say I was in love."

"Do you think you have to *say* it, Karin?"

Oscar was right. She didn't have to say it. All the people important, or close to her, guessed it without half trying. Mindy Lewis, who was becoming Karin's best girl friend now that they practiced basketball every day and lived fairly near each other, said: "Karin, I'd be jealous of the way Eric Ringquist looks at you if it weren't for one thing. I know he doesn't stand a chance. All anyone has to do is see the way you look at Steve Fletcher to know that."

Eric tried to be light and humorous about it. He was still Karin's shadow at school, waiting for her after classes, walking through the halls with her. And it was Eric, not Steve, who took her out to dinner once in a while, and to movies. Yet he was smart enough to "get the pitch," as he put it. "I've got the grandfather," he said several times, grinning, "but Steve's got the girl." Eric summed it up. "Maybe I'd stand a chance with the girl who's important to me, if her grandfather'd stop inviting me to dinner."

Her grandfather was annoyed about her friendship with Steve — because it was not what he had planned — but he tried to be tactful. The result was half comical, half irritating to Karin. "Gramp's about as subtle as a rattler shaking his rattles!" she commented to Ozzie.

This was true. He made all sorts of excuses for throwing Karin and Eric together. Little family parties were arranged. Eric's name was constantly on her grandfather's tongue, what a fine boy he was, how steady, how reliable,

51

how ambitious, what a good living he would make someday. He never ran Steve down, he merely tried to ignore
him into oblivion.

It irked her grandfather, and Karin knew it, that she
had such a valid excuse for seeing Steve so often. Yet he
could not object to her going over to the Fletcher barn for
basketball practice. Basketball was his baby, wasn't it?
He wanted a good team, didn't he? So Karin went — with
her grandfather's blessing despite the clouded look in his
eyes.

Evenings when she had finished her special coaching
sessions with his sister, Steve would come down and talk
if she could not stay late on account of homework. Then
there were other evenings when, her homework finished,
she was free to spend some time in his studio.

Nostalgia played its part in her relationship with Steve,
for where else in Rockridge could she breathe in the atmosphere that she had grown up in. No other place made her
feel so much at home. It was a complex emotion she felt
when she stepped into his studio, a compound of homesickness and well-being. Her eyes lingered upon the canvases, her nostrils drew in the familiar smells of paint and
turpentine. She could walk over to one of Steve's paintings
and rub her fingers over the surface and feel the spring-
iness of the canvas, the rough texture of paint hurled on
with a brush or slashed on with a palette knife.

Then there was the quiet of the place, the ineffable quiet
of an artist's studio where sound is hushed and one can
think.

They had their noisy times too. Steve was an eager con-
versationalist. Karin had never run into this in a boy, a boy
who wanted to sit her down in a chair and talk, talk for
hours on end. About ideas, visions, and dreams, about what
life is and what it ought to be, about books and plays and

artists and writers and just plain people.

Karin found herself faced with a new experience. For the first time she was in love with the *mind* of a boy.

Sometimes they listened to music or danced to the strains of the radio or record player. They danced well together, as two people do who are attuned to each other.

Still, underlying their friendship, was an unknown quantity that baffled Karin.

This unknown quantity was Steve himself.

Steve did not want to go out, to mix with the crowd. On the rare occasions when she managed to get him to a party, he would, as often as not, become the life of the place, thumping out jazz. He could be lots of fun. But it was like pulling teeth to get him there in the first place.

Usually it was Eric who squired her to parties — and there were many in this small Midwestern town! Eric was always ready to go, but Steve withdrew and if Karin put on the pressure, he became mulish.

" I've got more important things to spend my time on," was Steve's stubborn answer.

He was equally adamant about girls basketball. Karin came to regard it as his pet peeve. At the drop of a hat, Steve would sound off about it. He couldn't see why so much fuss was made over it out here. Sure he was proud of his sister and her ability to train girls in sports. She had coached championship teams back east. She was tops in her field. But why all the hullabaloo out here? He hadn't wanted her to take this job in the first place. It had been hard to pull up roots and start all over again. Now just because she had run into bad luck last year with her team, a hornet's nest of criticism was buzzing about her ears. It wasn't fair. She hadn't been given half a chance. He was fed up with the whole thing.

At school, despite his attractiveness and sometimes

charming manners, he was endangering his own popularity with the students and not helping his sister one bit. If only he could have kept quiet! But Steve could never hold his tongue, not when he had opinions, and he had them about girls basketball, violent and angry ones, which he talked about at every chance.

The chance came often, because girls basketball was the hottest topic at Rockridge High School these days. It was surrounded by conflict, with overtones of rivalry and competition that echoed throughout the county and the state. Rockridge just had to do better in basketball this year — or else. It was no fooling matter. The drama burst the confines of the high school walls and spilled over into civic affairs, the P. T. A., politics, and the press.

The press especially!

Karin pored over Sean Daly's summary of the Rockridge High basketball situation in the *Greene County Chronicle*.

"On Friday, Rockridge meets Red Creek for the first big blow in girls basketball this year. They meet in the Rockridge gym. It's a safe guess that every citizen of both towns who can drive, walk, or crawl to that game will get there.

"Rockridge is the underdog. The team had a bad season last year and a slow start this year. Yet it's hard to understand why.

"The Rockridge material is good. Carla Peterson, captain, is an aggressive forward with a powerful shoulder shot. Mindy Lewis has an uncanny way with rebounds and a sure eye for her special scoop shot. Babs Fairchild is a good all-court shot. The guards, Sue Harris, Deedie Rice, and Liz Ekstrom, can be fast and put up a fine defense when they want to.

"Then what's the trouble? From where we're sitting, it seems to be a lack of team spirit. While the school spirit

54

runs high, it seems at times as if this team does not *want* to win.

"Incidentally, their coach has come in for considerable local criticism, and this is not good for any team. Our own observation has been that Miss Fletcher — even though she does happen to be a woman coach — knows what she is doing. Given half a chance, we feel she might surprise everyone!"

"Our prediction for Friday night? Red Creek will clobber Rockridge right up into outer space."

CHAPTER | 6

KARIN STOOD in the circle of girls surrounding Miss Fletcher. They were crowded into the physical education office, listening to the coach name the line-up for tonight's game. When she finished, she looked at Karin and said, "You'll sit with the substitute forwards."

For a split second Karin felt a sharp pulse beat of pleasure at the announcement. Until now she had wondered whether Miss Fletcher considered her a good enough shot for even the substitute string. Then the pleasure was quickly replaced by dismay. Suppose I have to get out there on the court and play in front of three thousand people!

This was the first time she had ever played basketball at night. It gave an eerie strangeness to everything. The noise in the corridors was deafening. Above it Miss Fletcher's voice gave incisive last-minute instructions. The girls tried to pay attention, but their nerves were edgy. They wanted to be out on the floor. The signal came to go. Karin took a deep breath, braced herself. The crowd pushed against her, shoving her out into the hall.

Then that moment of utter silence as Rockridge in their hunter green uniforms stepped aside to let Red Creek, in scarlet, run ahead of them into the gym.

Screams, hoots, howls. Wild cheering. Whistles. The measured beat of cheerleaders' voices, rasping, strident. The smell of popcorn and peanuts.

Karin, panicked by her first appearance before the packed grandstand, wanted to turn and run. Someone nudged her and she ran across the court to the line of forwards warming up. She moved in the line, felt the sting of the leather as the ball was heaved at her, hurled it toward the basket. She did not watch or count her shots. She was too scared, an automaton, catching, lifting, heaving, dodging, running.

Now the captains stood in the center for the toss. Red Creek won. Their captain, a lean girl with an auburn ponytail, chose center throw on second and fourth quarters.

Karin stood with her team as the national anthem was played. Then she took her place on the bench, watching. The whistle blew. The referee hefted the ball into the air and tossed it to Carla Peterson. Carla caught it. She feinted to the right, the left, scanning the Rockridge side for an opening to Babs or Mindy. Both were covered by strapping guards, but Carla tossed to Babs. Babs caught it on the jump, stamped right, left, then right again, dribbled for a strategic aim at the basket. She let go a neat overhand hook pass to Carla, under the basket.

Then it happened. Karin, watching intently, blinked in disbelief. Babs's guard tapped the ball on an interception and shot it with adroit skill to Carla's guard. Carla jumped for it but missed. Red Creek had the ball.

Karin sucked in her breath. She had never seen anything like this in a girls game. That tricky play by Red Creek

56

would have had the referee's whistle blasting into the game back home. Or would it? She wasn't sure. It might have been a foul; maybe not. It had been so cleverly carried off she could not be sure. That was the trick, the special something Red Creek had.

The stands howled and roared as the ball went over to Red Creek. Karin hunched forward, watching. The Red Creek forwards passed the ball back and forth. Their feinting and timing were perfect. Karin saw they used a reverse pivot that gave them an advantage over the towering Rockridge guards. In less time than it took Karin to size up the play the captain dropped the ball into the basket.

A howl of triumph from the Red Creek side of the stands. Cheerleaders stamping on the gym floor. Who do we like? Adams, Adams, Adams. Who are we for? Team, team, team. What're we gonna do? Win, win, win.

Karin watched the girl named Adams flip her reddish pony tail with a conceited gesture. Her strut was self-assured as she took her place, hands on hips, near the mid-line. Karin's eyes swerved from the cocksure captain of the Red Creek team to her own side. Her friend Mindy was grim and worried. Babs looked jittery. Even Carla, solid as a monument, showed a tense jaw line.

The thought that edged into Karin's consciousness was one she tried to repulse. *They're licked already.*

On the next play she was sure of it.

The referee tossed Carla the ball. She passed to Babs nearby. Babs got away from her guard this time and hook passed to Mindy in the clear near the basket. Mindy aimed with an overhead shot and lost her balance; the ball caromed off, but Mindy was there for the rebound. She darted back, undecided between her scoop shot and a pass to Babs, chose the latter and let go with a pivot pass. Babs's guard went into a contortion that reminded Karin of one of those revved up movie shots, moving so fast all you can see is arms and legs. She came out of the struggle with the ball.

Karin half rose from the bench. She was surprised to hear her own voice roaring above the tumult in the gym. "Hacking! Personal foul! That was hacking!"

The game moved on. The referee's whistle did not stop it. The ball plunged across the dividing line toward Red Creek.

Karin heard her own voice screaming above the roars of the crowd as Red Creek made their second basket, and the scoreboard clicked up Visitors 4, Rockridge 0.

"Hacking! That was hacking!"

She felt a hand on her arm. Someone pulled her down. It was Ellie Thompson, another substitute forward. Overwrought, Karin spilled her wrath to Ellie.

"That guard hacked Babs!" she howled.

"No one could prove it," Ellie said. "And if you don't shut up, we'll be penalized for bad sportsmanship."

Karin sat there, chafing. Her stomach thumped as the game went on. Red Creek piled up a formidable number of shots. At the end of the first quarter the scoreboard read Visitors 16, Rockridge 4.

During the brief intermission, she turned to Ellie and raised her voice above the shouts of the cheerleaders. "I'd sure like to get into the game and show them a thing or two."

Ellie eyed Karin closely. "Boy, you sure are mad! I never saw you like this before. You're a different person."

"What our team needs is to wake up!" Karin shouted back. "Sure I'm mad. I'm mad at everybody. Red Creek, the referees, and our own kids. I should think they'd want to get together and lick the insides out of Red Creek after the tricks that bunch is pulling."

58

The whistle blew. The game went into the second quarter. Karin's fists clenched into tight knots. She thumped and thrashed and exploded inside. She couldn't do a thing. She was glued to the bench while Red Creek did what Sean Daly had predicted, clobbered Rockridge into outer space.

She slid from anger into dazed disbelief. Hoots and boos from the stands pummeled against her back. The Red Creek rooters, and some Rockridge ones too, were roaring their disapproval of the Rockridge team.

"Put away the slide rules, Rockridge! Toss out the psychology books. Hey, better get yourself a good man coach instead of a head shrinker."

Karin had to force herself to sit still. Time and again, she wanted to jump up and get into the game.

The buzzer rasped through her anger, announcing the end of the half. The scoreboard read 27–12. Karin watched the floor clear, saw the jubilant Red Creek girls run toward their coach. Rockridge walked tiredly off the floor. Then Karin was called to attention by a voice near her.

"Karin!"

She looked up and saw Miss Fletcher standing in front of her. "Do you think you could do anything to help this game?" the coach asked.

She jumped up. "I'd sure like to have a whack at it."

Miss Fletcher nodded. "I thought so," she said. "All right. Get in there next half and see what you can do."

The gym looked different in the blinding glare of the basketball court. Karin was nervous and anxious, blinking under the arcs of light. Her heart pounded hard, her hands trembled. The noise was deafening. Rising from floor to ceiling on all four sides of the vast gym she felt the swarming, pulsating presence of three thousand spectators.

She turned toward the boxed-off space reserved for city

59

fathers of Rockridge and families of the players. There she found Eric, waving to her, and Oscar and her grandparents. Her grandfather's towering frame and shock of white hair made him stand out even in that crowd. He waved his hand toward her in salute.

Maybe he's as frightened of this moment as I am, she thought.

She turned back to focus her attention on the referee. " Hey, Berglund," a voice shouted from the stands, "what are you gonna do out there? Show us how the bean eaters play basketball? " A wave of laughter and then another voice, " Hey, look, even her sneakers are new! "

She fixed her gaze on the stark white of her sneakers. It was true, they were brand new. What a mistake that had been, wearing new sneaks into this game!

The nasty crack shook her nervous system with the metallic insistence of a riveter.

" Even her sneaks are new! Even her sneaks are new! "

She heard Mindy's voice behind her. " Don't pay any attention, Karin. Miss Fletcher wouldn't have put you in if you weren't ready for it."

Mindy's encouragement was small comfort.

The whistle blew. Carla caught the toss and passed it to Mindy. Mindy sent it back to Carla who feinted to Mindy but passed to Karin. Karin jumped for it over the head of her five-foot-eleven guard. The impact of leather stung her finger tips. She held the ball lightly, turned, took aim, then let the ball sail toward the basket in a bank shot. It caromed against the backboard and sank through for a score.

Pandemonium from the stands. The megaphoned shouts of Rockridge cheerleaders. Give one for Berglund. Give one for Berglund, rah, rah, rah.

Two minutes before she had been the bean eater from

the East, the goon with brand-new sneaks. Now it was: Give one for Berglund.

" They'll think it's a lucky fluke," Mindy's voice was close behind her. " Show them it wasn't."

It hadn't been luck, and she knew it. It had been two things, that deadly aim which came from perfect vision, and Miss Fletcher's smartness in making use of this.

The ball was in play again, zooming toward the Red Creek side. Their captain caught it, dribbled, passed to a forward near the basket. Another time Red Creek would have had it all their own way. Now, braced by the skill Karin had shown in that first shot, the Rockridge guards perked up. They got the ball and sent it back over the line to Rockridge territory.

Mindy caught it. She pivoted, dribbled, feinted for a pass, then paused, holding the ball in both hands.

She's going to scoop-shoot it, Karin thought.

Mindy did. She darted back from the basket and released the ball with a scooping motion as she turned toward the basket. It came as a surprise to the guard. The shot was a clean one, dropping in for another quick score. Karin glanced at the scoreboard as it clicked the tally. Visitors 27, Rockridge 16.

Screams from the stands. The ball in play, fast, a furious pace as Red Creek sought to keep it and score. Again the aggressive attack from the Rockridge guards. Again the ball came over the line toward the Rockridge forwards. Karin caught it. She pivoted and aimed for another bank shot, but her guard balked her. There was a violent contortion, but this time the referee's whistle blew. The official's arm waved, hacking the air, sawing her own forearm. Personal foul in the act of shooting. Two free throws.

" Take it, Karin," Carla's voice commanded.

Karin winced. This was the moment she had been dreading. It was one thing to aim for the basket when you were in the heat of the game. It was another to stand at the foul line and drop that ball into the basket with the stands and the players holding their breath for you.

She stepped up to the foul line, moving slowly, her head down, her arms dangling. The referee handed her the ball. Her palms were moist. She wiped them on her shorts, one at a time, shifting the ball first to one hand, then to the other. Now she held the ball between her finger tips. No, loosen up, for pete's sake, let go!

Take your time, bean eater, she told herself. This is one deal you don't try to rush.

She raised the ball, paused, then sent it spinning toward the backdrop. It hit the spot she had aimed at and dropped neatly in. A howl of disbelief from the spectators. Again the referee handed her the ball.

Who could place a shot like that twice? She could feel the question bouncing against the walls of the vast gym.

The stands were restless. Red Creek rooters shouted that she could never make it. She shrugged off the noise. Finger tips on the ball, easy, easy does it. Broaden your base on this one. Last time your stance was a little cramped. There that's better.

Now, now let go.

The ball sailed high, going into the basket in a clean swish. Bedlam from the stands. Groans from Red Creek. Cheers from Rockridge. The rasping voices of cheerleaders, the rhythmic stomping of their feet in that fetish dance they did. Karin's teammates clapping her on the back. "Good work, Skeets! Nice going!" The whistle calling them back to the game. She had time to glance at the scoreboard.

Visitors 27, Rockridge 18.

From then on things happened so fast that she had no time to think, much less watch the scoreboard or listen to the thunder from the stands. The game took on a maddening pattern. Karin was in it, in it up to her neck.

This was basketball, as she had never played it. These Red Creek girls were tops in physique, drive, playing form. They used every trick in the bag, and they were fighting for their lives.

So was Rockridge. It became a kind of struggle for survival, a primitive thing that stirred emotions in Karin she had not even known she possessed. She wanted to win. She had to win. Winning was the one thing that counted.

She focused her eyes and mind on one thing, that ball, that brown sweaty thing that she had to get hold of, to hang on to, to put through that metal rim at any cost.

The cost was great. She was playing with everything she had, with taut nerves and strained muscles and a brain that was so pressured it wanted to explode.

Her palms were sore. Her breath came in short, spasmodic gasps. There was a kink in her right leg, but she ignored it. She was dripping wet, but she paid no attention to her body. The important thing was to keep her eye on that ball and get hold of it. Then aim it straight for the basket.

At the end of the third quarter she threw herself face down on the floor, her shoulders heaving, her breath coming in short, jerky sobs. It was a kind of agony that she wished would end, and yet not end. Her aching muscles were screaming to be taken out of the game, yet she wanted to stay in. Someone threw a coat over her. She didn't even glance up to see who it was.

" What's the score? " she gasped.

She heard Carla Peterson's voice answer her.

" 36-32. They're still ahead, Skeets." She felt Carla's arm on her shoulder. " You're doing a swell job." She nodded her thanks, keeping her face down, trying to control the heaving of her shoulders.

"Think we can lick them?" she asked.

"I don't know," Carla, ever the realist, spoke slowly. "Half hour ago I would have said never. Now, maybe. They're going to fight like bulldogs during the last quarter, and they've got the advantage of the throw."

The buzzer sounded. Karin pulled herself slowly up. The heaving shoulders were quieted. She felt better. Miss Fletcher stood at the side of the court watching her. Their glances met and the coach nodded, smiling. Not a word about quitting, on either side.

Carla had been right. The last quarter was for blood. The Red Creek team played as if their lives depended upon it. So did Rockridge. Arms, legs, bodies twisted and wrenched, flying through space on a jump. Again the taut nerves and aching muscles. Again the brain that wanted to explode.

Rockridge was playing clean basketball, fast, furious basketball, with their minds as well as their bodies, but it was clean. Red Creek had no choice but to follow suit because Rockridge had the edge on them. They had something Red Creek did not have, a forward who dropped in the ball every time she got it and took aim at the basket.

In the last minute of play the score stood tied, 42–42. It was Carla Peterson, not Karin, who broke the tie. She got the ball close to the dividing line and let go one of her famous shoulder shots. It plopped through, swishing the net just as the buzzer closed the game.

It was twenty minutes before Karin could get to the dressing rooms for her shower. She had first to withstand the barrage of congratulations that poured on her from every side.

She felt tired, terribly tired, with an ache that went deeper than muscles or nerves and brain, that went to the very core of her, a kind of soul tiredness.

64

Her grandfather was at her side, beaming, his arm tight around her shoulders. Oscar was with him, trudging close by, his lanky body bent toward Karin, nodding. Eric was there too, walking a little ahead, twisting around, never taking his glance off her, and her grandmother had tears in her eyes. All the people Karin loved most were here beside her in this moment of victory. All but one. Everyone had been here this evening to see Karin pull her team out of the doldrums but Steve Fletcher.

And strangely enough, Steve was the one who mattered most of all.

CHAPTER | 7

A CHANGED atmosphere pervaded the next practice session of the Rockridge team. For the first time the girls seemed willing to buckle down and work together as a team. Karin sparked the whole team to a new and fresh outlook.

Something was happening to Karin too. After the Red Creek victory she gained an increasing zeal for the game. It was more than for kicks now. It gave her a feeling of power. It gave her, too, a feeling of being needed and wanted because everyone recognized what she was doing for the Rockridge team. She became a star forward and carried them on to victory in three succeeding games. Samson, Fort Tyrone, and Prairie City were not the biggest teams in the county, but for Rockridge, the underdogs, to shellac them was news, big news.

Sean Daly made a lot of it in his column.

Who's Eating Crow? was the title of his article.

" Just about everyone in Greene County, including this

reporter, is eating it. Well, the Red Creek game was close, but Rockridge did win it, and now they've swamped three other towns.

"The big thing that has happened to Rockridge is Karin Berglund. Whatever is driving this girl, we don't know, but it sure packs a wallop on the basketball court. Karin Berglund has fire and flourish and they seem to be contagious.

"Rockridge has plenty of rough going ahead. The force of the Berglund personality has carried them on to four straight victories. This sort of tactics is good so long as it remains a surprise, but the surprise must be worn pretty thin by now.

"Miss Fletcher has scored a point. It was she who was smart enough to ferret out the hidden talent on her team. Her methods are different from those of most coaches. She tests her girls, then shuffles them around until she's got them playing the right positions.

"She places more stress on brain power than on the bulldozing tactics of her predecessor. For a long time this proved a losing battle. Now the tide seems to have turned. Whether her methods of coaching will stand up in the tough competition of Greene County basketball remains to be seen.

"The big question now is: How long will Miss Fletcher's team of dead-reckoning shooters and brainy guards be able to bring home the bacon?"

Karin read the article, looking over Mindy's shoulder in the cafeteria.

"His name should be Doubting-Thomas Daly," Karin said. "A real trusting soul, this guy. He sure isn't completely sold on Coach Fletcher, is he?"

"Are you?" Karin glanced sharply from the article to her best friend. Mindy's face showed more doubt than her question.

66

"Sure I am. Look what she's done for me. I'd be nuts not to appreciate it. I never even dreamed I could shoot. She's discovered me and built me up and whacked away on me, pounding and cudgeling me into a pretty good forward. Aren't you sold on her, Mindy?"

"Sometimes yes, sometimes no."

"I thought you were pretty much on her side, even before the winning streak began."

"I was, I was." Mindy seemed disturbed. "But something's bothering me. I can't quite put my finger on it. Sean Daly kind of hints about it in this article. He's a smart guy. I think what he's trying to say between the lines is that we've caught a kind of success fever, from you, Karin. But that one girl can't carry a team on to success forever. Personality isn't enough. You play an inspired game, true enough. But what would ever happen to our team if for some cockeyed reason you suddenly lost that fire and flourish of yours?"

"You give me too much credit. And you don't give Miss Fletcher enough. It's her coaching, not me, that's going to carry this team along."

"How?"

"She knows how to handle her team. She reads girls like an open book. That's nothing to sneeze at. If that team would give her complete co-operation, I think she could do a lot better than Bo Jensen. I think she could get us a championship for Rockridge."

Mindy whistled. "Say, you really are on her side, aren't you?" She studied Karin carefully. "It couldn't be because you're head over heels in love with that brush-wielding brother of hers, could it?"

"It certainly could not! Steve has nothing to do with my faith in his sister's ability."

"All right, Skeets, calm down. Forget I said it. Let's not

67

get into an argument over something that only time can prove anyway."

So the conversation ended, but it left an unpleasant flavor in Karin's thoughts. Mindy's doubts troubled Karin, for if Mindy, who was reasonably loyal, wondered how long their winning streak would last, how must the other girls, a few of whom were still not sold on a woman coach, feel?

She fussed and fumed over it. It was so much on her mind that she talked about it to Eric on the way home from the movies.

" I sure got myself plunked down in an awful mess," she said. " The fellow who said ' Go west, young man,' must have lived before the time of girls basketball."

" What's troubling you, Skeets? You've been a regular clam all evening. Even that hair-raising whodunit couldn't perk you up."

" I'm worried. Maybe it's selfishness, but I can't help it. I liked changing to forward, making baskets, having the limelight and all that is a real kick. But now it seems the responsibility is being dumped on me. So long as I win, fine. Suppose I should go to pieces sometime? "

" You won't."

They walked up the path toward the kitchen door. The light was still on and through the glass Karin could see where her grandmother had set out two cups, two plates, and a foil-wrapped package of sandwiches and another of cake for Eric and her.

" Come on in," she said. " The matchmakers have been at work, preparing a table in the wilderness for their two little lovebirds."

He caught hold of her hand. " Skeets, I wish you wouldn't."

" Wouldn't what? " She looked into his face, surprised

to see that for the first time since she had known him Eric showed signs of hurt and anger.

"Don't kid about you and me." He had hold of her shoulders, gripping them hard. "I've taken about as much of it as I can stand." He was talking close to her ear. "I know it's Steve all the way with you, Karin. But I've got feelings too, and I'm crazy about you. You ought to know that by now." He stopped and she could see his lip tremble. Then suddenly he let go of her. "I think I won't come in tonight," he said. "Good night, Skeets. I'll see you tomorrow."

"Whew! Now what have I done!" she said as she watched him run out to the car and start it, turning it out toward the main road with an angry flourish. "I sure have let myself in for a lot more than I figured. Go west, young lady, go west, indeed!"

But, despite Eric's reassurance about basketball, she could not stop worrying. It was the attitude of some of the girls that bothered her. They had accepted Karin completely, but they had by no means gone all out for Miss Fletcher.

Karin wished she could talk it out with them, but she knew they would never listen. She saw something in Miss Fletcher the others did not see.

Others might spoof all they wanted to about Miss Fletcher's "head-shrinking" tactics, but Karin saw that the coach had an exceptional ability to analyze her girls and make the most of their qualities.

For instance, take Carla Peterson. Next to Karin, she was the heaviest scorer on the team. But while Karin was satisfied to tuck the shots away in steady, quiet confidence, Carla craved the spectacular. She liked nothing better than to get 'way out on the floor, even when it was not necessary, and heave her shots in a sensational arc.

69

Carla was fine, so long as things went her way. Cross her and she snarled. Karin watched Miss Fletcher tackle Carla in her uppity moods. While everyone else was giving her a wide berth or turning themselves inside out to please, Miss Fletcher ripped off the kid gloves and told Carla to snap out of it if she wanted to stay in the game. It worked.

Then there was Babs Fairchild. Babs could be the most aggressive player on the team. She bulled her way through every game. Sometimes it could be comical, but other times it was no laughing matter because Babs could go wild on the court. She was as strong as an ox and big as a horse and when she sailed across that court bent on anni-hilation, she usually flattened out everyone, including her-self. Babs fouled heavily. She seldom lasted through more than half a game. Miss Fletcher brought Babs in line by keeping her on the bench through a couple of games that she wanted very much to get into. It worked.

Mindy was a " doll " and everyone loved her, including Karin, but there was a certain meddlesomeness about Mindy that often caused trouble. As in the Prairie City game, when, minding everyone else's business as usual, Mindy suggested to Carla that she was using too many spectacular shoulder shots. Mindy was right, but it was none of her business. Carla resented it. They locked horns in the dressing room with a subsequent free-for-all in which every player on the team took sides. The entire Rockridge team was reprimanded by the officials for dis-orderly conduct while Mindy pouted and Carla played the game in a towering rage.

After that Miss Fletcher found a way of keeping busy-body Mindy doing things for her. She worked Mindy so hard that she had no time to meddle into affairs that were none of her business. Mindy was glad to do chores for Miss Fletcher that the other girls might have spurned. It gave her the feeling of importance that she wanted. Mindy was happy so long as she was doing something for somebody. It worked.

The guards too presented problems that Miss Fletcher had to handle. Sue Harris was a real puzzler, even to Karin. She was a tall girl, but it seemed she let every other girl outjump her. Why? Karin watched Miss Fletcher crack the whip about Sue's heels. She made her drill longer, throw harder, jump higher. Once she said: "Sue, you're always complaining because other girls have steady dates and you don't. Well, Sue, the other girls *work* at being interesting dates. You're too lazy to be any boy's steady girl."

After that Karin noticed that Sue was a lot more active both on and off the basketball court, and a redheaded basketball guard named Tim Harvey began waiting outside of classes and after basketball practice for Sue. It worked.

Deedie Rice required Miss Fletcher to reverse her usual warning to the girls to behave like ladies on the court. Deedie was cautious, mortally afraid of fouling. Miss Fletcher set Deedie against the roughest forwards on the second string to harden her up, and that worked too.

It was Liz Ekstrom, however, who presented the most knotty problem on the team. Karin did not scare easily, but she admitted there were times when she felt a vague, undefined fear of Liz. Perhaps it was because Liz was the one person on the team who seemed to resent Karin's success.

The explanation was simple. Liz had, as long as she played the game, wanted to be a forward. She had, in fact, been a substitute forward under Bo Jensen. When Miss Fletcher arrived, Liz had signed up for that position. The new coach had soon put an end to Liz's delusions that she could ever be a good shot. First, Miss Fletcher had demanded that if Liz was to play at all, she must wear glasses while on the court. And she was to play guard. She could become an expert guard, Miss Fletcher argued, because she had speed, drive, a foxlike intelligence.

But she was definitely to wear eyeglasses. This enraged Liz, whose pretty face was her most prized possession.

"I hate the things!" she would howl, tearing off the "frames," as she called them, the minute practice was over.

Liz found it easy to hate a lot of things, and she had never forgiven Karin not only for succeeding as a forward but for snatching the prize Liz had wanted for herself, Steve Fletcher.

It was rumored that Liz had once been invited to the studio, and that Steve had begun a portrait of her and then abandoned it. Steve, with his bluntness, his glaring lack of diplomacy, had permitted Liz no face-saving when he broke off.

"She took too much for granted," he was supposed to have told someone who told someone else and then someone else. "I was never really interested in her. She just happened to have an interesting face that anyone would want to paint."

Karin kept out of Liz's path as much as she could. The girl had ample reason to dislike Karin and she knew it. She was quite a bit like a volcano, inactive, but likely to erupt at any moment. It was this controlled wrath that frightened Karin most of all. When it gave way, when Liz finally blew her top, the upheaval was going to be a humdinger.

Karin spoke to Mindy about it, just once.

"You're building it up," Mindy said. "I've never seen Liz lose her temper."

"That's the dangerous kind. When they give way, they tear up the place."

"Forget it, Skeets. She's harmless."

72

"About as harmless as a cobra, a starving cobra at that."

Mindy laughed. "You should worry, with your knack of getting along with people. You can handle anything, Skeets. Why, if a cobra slid into this room you'd just say, 'You sit there, darling, while I go and take care of the diamondback rattlesnake and the water moccasin. I'll handle you when I get through with them.'"

"It's a grim joke you're making, Mindy. Even Miss Fletcher hasn't learned how to handle Liz. She's the one girl that smart coach of ours hasn't learned how to reach."

Mindy didn't reply. She couldn't because it was an uncomfortable statement of fact. Liz Ekstrom with her tight-lipped antagonism baffled even Miss Fletcher.

CHAPTER | 8

STEVE WAS DOING a portrait of Karin. Every moment she could spare she spent in the barn of the Fletcher house, for when she was not sitting for Steve, she was perfecting her game on the basketball court downstairs.

Despite her phenomenal shooting success, she still had plenty of practice ahead before she became the kind of forward she now wanted to be.

Karin spent hours on the barn court dribbling, pivoting, feinting. She practiced all kinds of passes with both hands until she had mastered them. She worked on every type of shot: hook, chest, jump, overhead, shoulder, one-hand push, underhand loop.

It was during these periods of intense drilling that she decided to specialize in two things, tip-in shots and foul shots. For the former, she had height, her unerring eye for the basket, a long reach. For the foul shots she had a special steadiness.

The tip-ins would give the team added strength because both Carla and Babs were at their best away from the basket on long shots. Mindy was good at rebounds, but she did not have the height for the tip-in shot.

There was no doubt in Karin's mind that if she could improve her already sensational ability to land a foul shot, she would be one of the most valuable players in the county. She knew games were often won or lost at the foul line.

So she worked hard, driving herself, never relenting until she was perfect at whatever skill she was striving for. If she had stopped to take stock, she might have been astounded at the transformation that was taking place. Once or twice she did stop to take a long look at herself, to ask: Am I the same girl who shied away from this game when I first came here? Now it seems almost the most important part of my life.

Almost but not quite. For there was Steve. There he was upstairs in his studio waiting for Karin to finish her special drills under the ever-watchful eye of his sister so she could climb the stairs and be with him.

She would rest before sitting for her portrait, slumping in one of the two club chairs in the sitting-room part of the studio. If Steve was painting, he would keep at it, with the slight apology, "I'm in the middle of something." If he wasn't, he would sit across from her and talk until she was ready to pose.

Steve was painting her in the dress she had been wearing when Eric had introduced them that day in the hall at school. "It's the way you looked when I really saw you for the first time," he said. "That was a red-letter day in my life, Karin."

74

So she kept the dress in what he called his sister's half of the barn, downstairs near the shower room. She would take her shower after her workout on the court, and Miss Fletcher would be there to help her into the dress, to hook it for her, smooth out the folds and pat her hair into place.

It was a dress of yellow wool, the color of pale jonquils in early spring, keyed just below the yellow of her hair. She wore no jewelry, but a pale blue stole flung about her shoulders picked up the color of her eyes.

"Swedish colors," she said to Steve. "Yellow and blue. You're painting me as a real *svenska!* It will please my grandfather."

Steve did not answer, but Karin understood that Steve knew it was Eric, not he, who was most welcome in the Berglund home, no matter what he ever did to please her grandfather.

Steve would never let her see the portrait, "not until it's finished," and he would throw a cover over it whenever she was in the studio. Yet she could tell from the way he handled his brushes that this would be in the same technique as Steve's other paintings, bold, free, modern.

So she was seeing him a lot. It seemed as if basketball and Steve, Steve and basketball formed the pattern of her life. This was not entirely true, of course, because her hours were filled with many other things. There was school that demanded much more than the classroom time she put in. She had to keep up in her studies and get good grades in order to stay on the basketball team.

Then there were her frequent dates with Eric. She had a new respect for him since that angry episode when he had asked her not to joke any more about their friendship. Whatever it was that had been bothering him that night had passed. He was his old good-natured self. But Karin knew now that Eric was in love with her, knew it for sure, and a boy in love seldom wanted to hear jokes about his feelings.

It was an odd set of circumstances that Karin found herself in, for she was almost going steady with Eric. They were a couple, invited together whenever there were dances and parties. Yet everyone knew that she was crazy about Steve, everyone perhaps but Steve himself.

For this was the most troublous part of her life these days, this relationship with Steve. She was a clearheaded girl, " sensible " everyone called her, including her grandparents, and for this very reason Steve baffled her. She simply did not know where she stood with him. What puzzled her most of all was that their friendship did not seem to progress, to get anywhere, as she put it.

Steve was always delighted to have her drop in at the studio. Occasionally, when his sister had evening meetings, Steve would take Karin to the Buxton Diner for a hamburger plate. This was fun because the Buxtons were as fond of Steve as if he were their own son. They gave Steve the run of the place, let him show them how coffee really ought to be made, saved his favorite pecan pie for him, kept a sketch he had made of Ma Buxton, dog eared and grease stained by now, pasted near the cash register.

Here Karin could relax with Steve and have fun, talking, listening to their favorite records on the jukebox. She would drive him back to the studio and he would kiss her good night in a more brotherly than romantic way, and she would go home, wondering. Was he just fond of her, as he might be of any girl, or did she mean more to him than just another date? Or was the first keen edge of pleasure in her company wearing off and was Steve, known for his fickleness, beginning to lose interest? Or had his true interest in her been, from the start, nothing more than intellectual, the companionship that must naturally spring up between two people who had similar interests and liked to talk about the same things.

She asked herself these questions, yet she never knew the right answers to them.

Steve still wanted her around, that was certain. He was keenly interested in the portrait he was doing of her. He asked her advice at every turn, about his work, his paintings. He pumped her dry about her father's techniques. He wanted her encouragement and her support and her comfort when things were not going right.

In fact, Steve was using her to the hilt, and she knew it, but she did not care. She was happy to be with him as much as he would let her be. She gave freely to him of her knowledge about painting. Like so many people who are not artists themselves, yet have been exposed to this life, she had developed a keen sense of criticism. So she could help Steve, help him lavishly in the thing that seemed most important to him.

Yet he was still to her what he had been from the start, a mystery, an unknown quantity.

Her relationship with her grandfather, on the other hand, was much clearer than it had been during those early days of her arrival. Sometimes she would hop in the station wagon or jeep with him and ride out to one of the farms. He loved having her company. If there was a thaw in the deep snows that blanketed the prairies, and the ground permitted it, they would ride on their horses, she on a tractable gelding named Ebony and he on a stallion named Demon.

Even now, at his age, he would ride nothing but a stallion, and he was still straight in the saddle. Karin felt closest to him during these moments because she got the full measure of her forceful grandparent, understood his drive and energy.

She remembered Mamie's early words to her, "You two are cut from the same stick of dynamite, the old one and the young one," and she could see now how true this was.

She liked to look at him when he mounted Demon, his sturdy frame clad in a worn tweed riding jacket and old plaid shirt, his white hair whipped by the wind, for he refused to wear a hat when he rode, his bronzed face, beaten by sun and wind and rain but remarkably free of wrinkles. He seemed eternally young in his movements, in his vigor and outlook on life. And Karin was learning at long last to talk with him, and he with her.

She wrote to her father about it, a long letter in answer to the first real letter she had received from him since his marriage. There had been post cards from their honeymoon trip and several short telephone calls to see how she was making out. Now at last there was a long letter, written half by Joan, half by her father, and they wanted her to tell them everything about her new life.

"Darlings, both of you," she began, "where shall I start? With basketball, I suppose, because it is the most exciting thing out here. You haven't any notion how big it is until you live here in the Midwest and smell, eat, talk, breathe nothing but basketball all winter! Then she brought them up to date on her own and Rockridge's progress.

"There are lots of other things to tell. I wish we could just sit down and talk about them. Let's see, people are the most fun to hear about, so here goes. Oscar, Gramp's right-hand man, has become a good friend. He listens to all my woes, let's me cry on his shoulder as often and long as I like. And he's always good for some down-to-earth advice when things aren't going the way they should.

"Eric's another good friend, a boy in my class, and he lives on the next farm (which means a lot farther away

78

than 'next door' back home!). Out here they call him my 'Friday night date,' which means we go to the movies or out to dinner once in a while and to school affairs.

"Then there's Mindy Lewis, the girl on the team who has become my best friend. Mindy's swell, cute, and pretty in a pixie-ish sort of way. Oh, she's a regular little busy-body, going around doing good deeds for people who'd rather be let alone, but anyway you'd like her a lot because she rings true.

"You wanted to know how I like living with Gramp and Grandma, with all this space to move around in. First, I didn't like it. You know what bothered me most of all? There was too much of everything! It sort of dazzled and confused me. Too much space outdoors, too much house inside, too many new clothes to keep shined up! Back home when we lived in our cottage with a station wagon (one — not five cars — yessiree, f-i-v-e, including the jeep), and I had a few dresses and some slacks, and the only thing we ever had too much of was cats and dogs — well, I used to have dreams then. I used to think, especially come the end of the month and the bills were piled up, I used to think then — wow! — if only we had more dough. Boy, would I go on a buying spree. I'd have lots of everything. I'd buy, buy, buy.

"Then all at once it happened. Here I was with everything I wanted and more. All I have to do is squeak one little wish or want and presto, Gramp goes running to get it. You know what? It didn't prove to be the great big kick I thought it might be. It reminded me of Jezebel, that old terrier of ours, and her bones. When she didn't get one, she'd yip and squeal. Give her bones, all she wanted, and what did she do? Go out and dig a hole and hide 'em.

"Another thing bothered me. I didn't like to keep accepting all this stuff, even from my own grandfather. Oh,

79

Gramp was swell about it, but he wanted to get me so much that I began to get a sticky feeling, sort of obligated.

"Well, we've worked out a lot of things. I think Gramp is beginning to understand me. We used to explode at each other once in a while — people say we're an awful lot alike!

"My interest in basketball — although I'll admit he twisted my arm at first to get me into it — has helped. Gramp even comes over to the Fletcher barn sometimes to watch me practice. He brings Oscar or Eric, and he just about busts his vest buttons with pride."

She paused in her letter writing. She had not yet mentioned Steve, and the last sentence brought him uncomfortably into her thoughts. Steve had not once come down while she was actually drilling. "Hands off this Midwestern brand of basketball for me!" was his only comment. His stubbornness about this and so many other things upset her.

There were so many loose ends where Steve was concerned that she hesitated to write about him. She might betray her true feelings and that would be unfortunate because Steve had certainly given her small encouragement to declare she was in love with him. Maybe this was just the difference between a girl and a boy. Perhaps the girl must always show more affection. No, that couldn't be it. There was Eric. If she so much as crooked her finger, she felt sure he would be ready to tell her how deep his feeling for her was. Eric loved her and she loved Steve and Steve — loved — ?

Maybe that was it. Perhaps love was always a thing in profile like the heads on those old Roman coins. The faces were all turned in the same direction, each looking at the one ahead. Maybe love was like that, each reaching out to the one ahead, who would not turn and reciprocate.

She picked up her pen and turned again to her letter.

"I have not told you about Steve yet. And honestly he's hard to write about because he's got so many different moods! He paints, and that makes me feel right at home with him, Dad, and you can understand why.

"He's doing a portrait of me. I haven't any idea how it'll turn out. He won't let me see it until it's finished. I can hardly wait!

"Sure, I can describe him for you if you like. He's taller than I am (he just better be!) and kind of skinny and good-looking if you like a face that's serious most of the time.

"I like him a lot but is he changeable, Dad! You never know what he's going to say or do next. I guess you could say he's got a pretty good opinion of himself because he likes to pick things to pieces, people, the way the world is, politics, books, anything. He isn't always right, but I don't tell him that! I let him sound off and string along, because how else are you going to get along with boys?"

She stopped. She had said enough about Steve. Looking back over the last few paragraphs, she smiled. "Who said that love is blind?" she spoke to her father's picture in the silver frame on her desk. "I've told you that Steve is self-willed, conceited, fickle, and critical. You'd never guess in a million years that I love him."

CHAPTER 9

AN AIR of cockiness hung over Rockridge High on the eve of the Grandville game. Even Sean Daly, that venerable skeptic, gave them the edge to win. Karin read his column, clipped and mounted on the bulletin board of the physical education ell.

" On Wednesday, the Rockridge girls face Grandville, their toughest opponents since Red Creek. Rockridge has proved itself to be a team that no sane sports commentator would try to dope out. But our forecast is fair weather and clear sailing for the girls in hunter green. Grandville has one of the best man coaches in the state, Skip Hennessy. But they were beaten by Red Creek who in turn was nudged out by Rockridge. If Grandville has drive, Rockridge has that big something called will to win. Providing this holds out, we prophesy they'll walk off with the game."

School spirit ran high. Wherever Karin turned at school she ran into posters pleading, begging, ordering the student body to come to the game and bring their families. The newspapers ran blatant advertisements. The entire school expected the girls to win, and none seemed more certain of victory than the girls on the team.

Karin had lunch with Mindy in the school cafeteria on the day of the game.

" I never felt so jittery before a game," she confided to her friend. " I don't know what's bothering me. Maybe it's all this cocksureness."

" Don't you think self-confidence is a good thing? "

" Yes, of course I do. But we're all acting as if it's in the bag already. You'd think we'd already won that game."

" I see what you mean, Skeets. But it's not our fault that

we're so sure. Everyone expects us to win. Even Sean Daly."

" He hasn't been at our last five practices."

Mindy did not answer. She knew very well what Karin was talking about. The last few practices had been horrendous. The trouble could be traced to several things. First, many of the girls had swelled heads over the Rockridge victories. They had climbed so steadily since the Red Creek game that some of the team felt they knew more about basketball than the coach. The second source of trouble was Miss Fletcher's coaching methods. At best, the girls disliked them; at worst they resisted them.

Miss Fletcher had been hired by Karin's grandfather to correct the roughhouse tactics of Bo Jensen. She took her assignment seriously. She had a few pet phrases that she used again and again. In the manner of schoolgirls the world over, these were picked up by her team and mimicked.

" Now, girls," and they would ape Miss Fletcher's dignified manner and low-pitched voice, " there does not have to be roughhouse if every movement is automatic in both execution and planning."

The girls on the team would repeat this instruction to one another amidst giggles in the locker room.

Or again, " Remember, girls, our subject is physical education, which means physical *plus* education." They would raise one finger in admonition as they said, " *plus* education," just as Miss Fletcher did. Then they would continue their take-off of the coach. " We start with a sound, efficient body, but our ultimate goal is also mental development. We must *think* as well as move! "

This last sentence, " We must *think* as well as move! " invariably brought down the house.

Karin did her share of the fun-poking. She was one of

the best mimics on the team. It was all done in fun, despite the underlying note of seriousness. No one was malicious; they would have died if the coach had discovered their shenanigans, but it did act as a kind of safety valve for their pent-up feelings. After all, Miss Fletcher's methods were tedious!

The key to Miss Fletcher's coaching technique was repetition. "I know of no other way to master the automatic control of every play and situation that may arise on the basketball court," she told the girls above their groans of protest. Her method was to set up floor situations and repeat them again and again, forcing the girls into habits of thought and movement that would meet these conditions.

"When you meet similar conditions in a game, you'll know how to cope with them instantly," she told her team.

So they practiced endlessly. For instance, they would take the immediate guard setup, the positioning of guards on the floor, following a rebound from the basket, and drill on it until they nearly dropped.

They did the same for positions and passes following the center throw. They worked on the out-of-bounds and jump balls until they wanted to scream for help. The forwards especially were rebellious because Miss Fletcher gave them a double dose of drilling, insisting not only on practice of passing and shots but drawing them into *defensive* practice, reversing the old saying that the best defense is offense.

"Never sail along on a purely aggressive game. Because an equally aggressive bunch of forwards on an opposing team will blast you right off the court, especially if their guards are high geared," she told them.

They worked, worked, worked. The girls griped. Miss Fletcher commanded respect, so although they did not like what she did, their dislike never became insolence.

Much of it was off-the-record grumbling as they got into their suits, wailing as they took their showers. They fretted and fumed. They kicked and criticized. They groused until they were blue in the face about the boredom of the coach's methods. This did not make their practices pleasant ones. Then a week before the Grandville game that incident occurred which made the following practices a veritable mockery. Karin, unfortunately, was in the dead center of the trouble.

It started, as major crises often do, with a small incident of no consequence whatsoever. Liz Ekstrom lost her sneakers.

Of all the girls, Liz was the least outspoken in the locker rooms. Her resentment toward Miss Fletcher was far more subtle than that of the other girls who kidded and ranted about the coach's unique methods. Yet her resentment smoldered. She didn't have to say or do a thing. Karin could see the hatred in Liz's eyes, narrowed to slits, whenever Miss Fletcher gave her an order.

The sneakers Liz lost were not even new ones. They were disreputable relics, pock-marked with age, dirty and worn from the many games they had slid and jumped through. But they were as important a possession to Liz as the bracelets awarded to the girls who won the state basketball championship.

Why? Because on the inner side of both sneakers, in indelible ink was printed the sentence, " Liz, I love you."

Liz swore the words had been printed there by Steve Fletcher. Steve neither denied nor confirmed Liz's assertion. He simply did not care. Karin, who knew about the far-famed sneaks with the sentimental inscription inside, thought it quite possible that Steve might have done this. In a mood of playfulness, when his wit was riding high, it might have seemed an amusing thing to do. He could do it and forget it the next moment. Karin knew that Steve was like this.

Whatever the truth about the incident might be, Liz loved those sneakers. She saved them for important games, like Red Creek and Grandville. She carried them back and forth to school in the leather feed-bag carryall, which she toted as a handbag. They were her amulet, Liz's protection against whatever devils she believed in. Anyone wise in the legends of Rockridge High School would have conceded that Liz Ekstrom would sooner have given up a good right arm than that pair of dirty old sneaks.

The afternoon that she stormed into the gym late for practice and announced that her sneakers were gone a hush fell over the team. Carla, in the act of tossing the ball in a hook pass to Karin, stopped dead in her tracks. So did Mindy and Deedie and Sue Harris. The substitute string on the benches got up and turned toward Liz. The place was so quiet you could hear the click of the wall clock as the minute hand jumped.

Liz repeated the sentence she had flung out. "I said somebody took my sneaks."

"Which sneaks, Liz?" Mindy asked the direful question for the rest of them. "You mean *the* sneaks?" Liz nodded. It was obvious she couldn't find the voice to answer. Her face was dark with wrath.

Mindy, ever helpful, walked over to Liz. "Why, no one could have taken them, Liz. What would anyone want to do that for? They wouldn't be worth anything to anyone but you."

Liz found her voice. "Karin Berglund knows where they are."

Karin's mouth dropped open. "Me? I never laid hands on them in my life."

Liz faced her. Karin was astonished at what she saw in

Liz's expression. It was more than animosity, it was an obsession. All the smoldering hatred of which Liz seemed capable flared up. It twisted her features, making a stony mask of her face.

Miss Fletcher stepped between them. " Come on, girls. We've had enough of this. Liz, your sneakers are bound to turn up. Karin, get with the ball."

Liz was not so easily put off. " She's jealous of me." Her voice echoed through the gym, bouncing against the walls. *She's jealous of me. She's jealous of me.*

Karin tried to get away from the echo, but there was no place of escape. She had to face the irate Liz.

" Steve Fletcher liked me more than he does her and she knows it," Liz's normally quiet voice took on the resonance of anger. " He's just using her, and she knows that too. She wanted to destroy those sneaks because of what was printed in them. She can't fool me with her smiles and sweet ways. I can see right through Karin Berglund."

Karin recoiled. She drew back from the battering impact of Liz's anger. All around her Karin heard the gasps of her teammates and Mindy's voice saying, " Oh, come on, Liz, be yourself."

Miss Fletcher's sharp command cut through the jumble of voices. " I said break it up, girls."

They broke it up and everyone but Liz returned to the game, but the damage had been done. Practice that afternoon was a total loss. Even Miss Fletcher, whose iron-hand-in-the-velvet-glove got perfect discipline, could not force them into her routine of drill and repetition.

Karin was stunned. She was afraid of Liz, of what she might do. Karin was sure, like Miss Fletcher, that the sneaks would turn up. But the hatred she had seen in Liz's face!

Karin saw Liz Ekstrom as she really was for the first

time. This was the girl who defied penetration, who until now had cleverly evaded revealing herself. If the sneakers, precious talisman that they were to Liz, had not been lost, she might never have given herself away.

Now Karin saw and knew. This girl was unwilling to face reality, and therefore dangerous. She would believe only what she wanted to believe, and she wanted to convince herself that Karin had taken those sneakers. Even if they turned up she would still go on believing that Karin had taken them.

Her thrust had been deadly and accurate. " Liz reminds me of a hungry cobra," Karin had once told Mindy, and Mindy had joked about it.

Now the cobra had struck home, to the core of Karin's relationship with Steve. Where would it strike next?

Buffeted by these thoughts, Karin went through the automatic motions of the practice game, doing what Miss Fletcher told them to do.

But her heart was not in it. Not that day or the next or the next. The entire team knew it. They were restless and uneasy. They complained and bickered among themselves. The tension between Liz and Karin spread to the rest of the team. Karin knew what was happening, but somehow she could not shake herself out of her own mood, much less do anything to perk up the others.

Then, on the day before the Grandville game, she was confronted by the double risk to which her team had exposed itself. They had frittered away that valuable week of practice before a big game. Yet they were cocksure, puffed up with previous success. They were the team who had begun as the underdogs, rallied and plunged on to victory after victory.

They were unbeatable. Everyone said so, and they themselves were convinced of it.

88

KARIN PULLED into the parking lot outside the high school. She nosed the car into the last space in the section reserved for the basketball teams.

Whew! she thought. Of all nights to be late, I sure picked the worst. Miss Fletcher is going to have fits.

The coach had given strict orders that everyone was to be there a half hour early for a team meeting before the game. It had been obvious to Karin all week that while the team was heady with success, sure of victory, Miss Fletcher was on tenterhooks about the Grandville game.

Karin hurried across the lot, watching her footing, sliding on the icy spots. It was a perfect night for the game, as far as the weather went — bright, with a moon sailing high, cold but clear. The turnout would be terrific, a packed house for sure.

" Hi! " she called to friends as she hurried on. " Am I in a hurry! I'm going to catch it. Gangway, everybody," she shouted to the crowd at the head of the stairs.

Laughter followed her down the stairs. " Skeets," someone called after her, " wham them in good tonight. We're banking on you."

" I'll do my best," she called back.

She flung open the door of the physical education office where the girls had been instructed to meet. The moment she stepped into the room, she felt that something was wrong. Miss Fletcher merely nodded to her as she slipped into the last seat near the door.

Karin sat on the edge of the chair, unwinding her plaid scarf from her head and shoulders, twisting out of the sheep-lined coat.

What's wrong? she thought. What's going on here? Miss Fletcher's face looked drawn, almost white in the artificial light, and her mouth was a thin line of worry and displeasure. Then Karin looked around at her teammates and got some inkling of what the trouble was.

Most of the girls were slumped in their seats with that empty stare that indicates a total vacuum where the mind should be.

They're bored stiff, Karin thought. And it's written all over their faces. No one's listening to a word Miss Fletcher is saying.

She wasn't especially interested herself. It was old stuff by now and all of them had heard it again and again.

Miss Fletcher's voice hammered away at the team. "You've been given the idea that Grandville will be an easy team to beat this year. Don't forget one important fact, that no team is beaten until you've defeated it." There was a restless stirring among the girls.

Karin could almost feel their thoughts: "Oh, turn it off. We've heard this kind of corny pep talk before."

Miss Fletcher went on. "We'll use the figure-eight attack at the start of the game. Remember, this is based on working the ball down in a fairly straight line toward the basket. The guards must be in on the play as much as the forwards. You know our system: A good defense is what makes an offense possible."

"Corny," someone muttered. Karin was not sure which one of the girls had muttered the word, and she could see that Miss Fletcher had not caught the mumbled criticism. But Miss Fletcher's ears pricked up at the snickers that came from the girls who were near enough to hear.

"What's the joke?" she asked. There was no answer. Several of the girls pulled themselves up to attention. Miss Fletcher looked around the group. Karin saw the pulse beat in her jaw, the way her hands gripped the back of the desk chair as she stood near the board on which she had placed her floor-play diagrams. Karin felt she knew this woman better than any other girl on the team. They had worked closely together for long hours during Karin's transformation from guard to forward. What she read in the coach's face at this moment troubled her. She had never seen her so upset before. The importance of this game, the attitude of the girls, heaven knows what pressures from the town and the recreation committee had built up inside this usually calm woman.

She looks ready to blow her stack, Karin thought. I sure hope she holds off till after the game.

Apparently Miss Fletcher decided to let the wave of snickers pass without further comment. She turned back to the board, chalking out further instructions. Most of the girls were alerted to Miss Fletcher's mood and had changed their behavior, outwardly at least. Karin noticed that they had improved their postures and were making an effort to appear interested.

Miss Fletcher's voice droned on, saying the things she had said a hundred times before. Then she concluded her instructions to them.

"I want you to remember one thing, if nothing else. It's all summed up in two words, *Be there.*"

As the final words, "Be there" left Miss Fletcher's lips, a hysterical laugh broke out in the room. Everyone turned toward Liz Ekstrom. She was bent forward, her head in her hands and her body was shaking. Her laugh, almost eerie in tone, filled the room. Miss Fletcher walked down to where Liz was sitting.

"What's the matter with you, Liz?" she asked.

"I — can't — help — it," Liz wheezed out the words through a fresh outburst of laughter. "It's funny."

"What's funny?"

"The way you keep saying '*Be there.*'"

It was true that Miss Fletcher kept saying these words, and it was true that by now they had a comical meaning through endless repetition. "Be there," she had said so often that the girls wanted to escape from the order. "This means be at the right place, at the right time, doing the right thing. You can't miss if you manage to *be there.*"

Liz continued to laugh hysterically. Miss Fletcher's pulse beat was showing again in her jaw line. She flushed, then drained to that strange whiteness again.

"Liz, if you can't control yourself, perhaps I'd better keep you out of the first quarter of this game."

Liz choked down her laughter. She got up. Karin watched her. Liz's eyes were overbright; two spots of color stood out on her high cheekbones.

"Why does everyone always pick on me?" her voice was shrill.

Here we go, Karin thought. This is the blowup Liz has been threatening to give us for a long, long time.

She did not wait for an answer. "First my sneaks were stolen and now tonight it's my fault if I can't help laughing. Well, it's not my fault. I didn't start this. Everyone knows who started it."

"What are you talking about?" Miss Fletcher asked. "Who started what?"

"I mean that song. The one about the way you always tell us to 'Be there.' I didn't make up that song." She whirled around and faced the spot where Karin was sitting. "Karin Berglund's the best mimic on the team. She's the one who makes all the jokes about the things you say and the way you talk and the way you repeat things over and over again. She's the one who made up that song."

Miss Fletcher's voice sounded as upset as she looked.

"I don't think I've had the pleasure of hearing that song," she said icily.

Liz shoved back her chair, getting out into the aisle. She executed a few dance steps, swinging into a jive tune as she did so. Her voice was strident, tuneless, and deadly as she thumped out the song: "Be there, ye high and mighty forwards. Be there, ye low and lazy guards. Now all you high-stepping leather pushers, you better just be there!"

There was stark silence in the room when Liz finished. Karin felt herself break into a cold sweat. She wanted to duck, to hide, to escape, but there was no way to do it where she sat, in the blazing overhead lights of the small office.

Miss Fletcher was staring at her, her face full of disbelief.

"I — I just can't believe this, Karin," she said, stammering over the words. "I can't believe you'd do anything like this."

Karin got up. Her knees shook, her hands were cold. She tried to find her voice in her parched throat, but no sound came, not right away. Her thoughts tumbled over one another in fear and confusion and shock. She was guilty and yet, she was not guilty. She had made up that song, true enough, but it had been in fun. It had seemed all right at the time. All the girls had been cavorting around the locker room, poking fun at the coach's methods and mannerisms and way of speaking. It hadn't been only Karin. It had happened that Karin was the wit of the team, the one who was quickest with the wisecracks.

Yet, how could she explain all this to the shocked and angered woman who now faced her, a woman who seemed like a stranger to Karin rather than the close friend she had proved to be.

It was Mindy who stepped into the breach for Karin.

"Miss Fletcher," she said, getting up and going over to where the coach stood. "It wasn't Karin's fault. We were all in on it. Karin made up the song, but we all danced to it. We all thought it was funny. If you're going to punish anyone, it better be the whole team."

A groan went through the room. Good old Mindy had really cooked their goose this time.

"Oh, Mindy," Carla exclaimed, "why can't you keep your big mouth shut?"

"I'm only trying to help," Mindy lashed back at Carla.

Miss Fletcher separated them. She stood there in the silence in the room, looking from one to another of her team. The girls glanced away, unable to face the accusation in the coach's face.

"So you all were in on it," she said. "You all thought it was funny. My methods are a joke to you." No one answered.

Miss Fletcher paused, then swept on. Her voice was calm and steady despite the suppressed emotion back of it.

"For the last five days, you've been going through the motions of playing basketball, the motions only. You've paid no attention to anything I've said. Now I can see why. Then tonight you've come in here riding the crest of the wave. You're sure no team can beat you and you think you're good enough to beat Grandville without any help from anyone, even a coach. Well, let me tell you, Grandville is no pushover."

She paused, then continued, her voice even more calm.

"You may not realize it, but I haven't been hired by the town of Rockridge to knock my head against a stone wall, trying to convince this team that my way of coaching is right."

She stopped, letting that sink in.

"If I didn't believe it was right, I wouldn't have tried

it in the first place. But it seems you have other ideas. You're all very sure of yourselves. You don't need me. You are a team capable of going out on that basketball court and licking the stuffing out of Grandville on your own."

Her eyes swept the group, and now they were blazing although the voice was still steady and quiet.

"So I'm going to let you do just that. You're on your own, 'my high and mighty forwards, my low and lazy guards.'" She was staring straight at Karin as she repeated the words of that horrible little song. "You're on your own."

She started toward the door. Carla stepped in front of her. "Where are you going, Miss Fletcher?" she asked.

"I'm going up to the bleachers, to the highest seat I can find. I'm going to lose myself and let you play this game alone."

She walked out, leaving the door open behind her. The silence in the room was abysmal. Gone the restlessness, the boredom, the cocky self-assurance. Karin shivered. It was bad enough for the others, they had lost a coach. But she was the one who had made up that song about the woman who had helped her so much. She had lost both a coach and a friend.

CHAPTER 11

ON THE FLOOR of the Rockridge gym, the Grandville team looked formidable, not at all the pushovers everyone had declared they would be.

Karin's team was using part of the warmup period for a confab. Carla had them at the side in a huddle. She looked worried as she outlined the strategy for the opening quarter of the game. The rest of the team was silent.

" I don't like this any more than the rest of you," she said. " But we got ourselves into it, and we'll have to do the best we can."

Karin might have been frightened of the prospect of playing a game without Miss Fletcher to guide them, if she had been given time to think about it. Once on the court, the pace, even during warmups, was too fast for much thought. When the huddle broke up, she ran over, taking her place in the line of forwards practicing shots at the Rockridge side. As the line moved along she searched the stands as she did before every game. She found her grandparents, Oscar, and the Ringquists. She waved and moved up quickly to take her turn at the basket. Her hands could have been steadier. She fumbled the first shot, and it bounced off the rim.

" Whassamatta, Berglund? " someone shouted from the stands. " You handled that one like a greased pig."

There was some laughter. It did not bother her. She was troubled by something more serious than the heckling from the stands. Where was Miss Fletcher? Her eyes traveled up, up the towering mountain of the stands. Up there were only heads and faces and arms and legs.

She moved along the line of forwards. Her throat was

dry, her hands felt cold and nervous. Get hold of your emotions, she told herself. Carla's right. We're in the mess — and it is a mess, for sure — we'll have to get out of it.

She saw the ball arch toward her from the hands of the substitute forward ahead of her. She caught it on the jump, aimed, paused, sent it spinning toward the rim. It went in, a clean shot.

Run, run, take your place in line, she told herself. Get ready for the next sting in your palms, the next thrust toward the backboard. You're an old-timer at this now. You almost never miss. You can do it without thinking.

She did. She went through the warmup without missing another shot. The stands were backing her up. "Atsa stuff, Berglund. Nice going, Skeets. Wham them in, Karin. You know how!"

Rockridge won the toss. A good omen. Karin's spirits began to pick up, her nerves to mend. Maybe the going wouldn't be so bad after all.

The excitement of basketball gripped her as it had in previous games. It was a sense of power, of knowing that whenever that ball came to her, providing she kept her eyes open and her nerves steady, she could put it through that netting. It was something more than this too. It was a spirit of confidence and gumption that had carried her team along with her. People called it different things, enthusiasm, drive, the will to win.

She didn't give it a name. But she felt it, felt it so strongly that even the concern over Miss Fletcher could not suppress this driving force.

The buzzer cut into her thoughts. She heard the whistle, saw the ball whip from the center forward through the air toward the Grandville side. One of their forwards caught it, feinted, pivoted, sent the ball hurtling to another forward who passed it quickly to a basket hanger. Liz, guard-

97

ing, blocked a shoulder shot. Forced to get rid of the ball, the forward sent it high over Liz's head to the captain of the team. Sue Harris blocked this one and the captain heaved the ball back to the basket hanger. This time the girl succeeded in ducking Liz and the ball hefted in an underhand shot for the basket.

It bounced in and the scoreboard clicked two points for Grandville.

Karin looked at Mindy and shook her head. It had been a quick, easy score. Too quick and too easy. Liz and Sue had guarded but not with their usual tenacity or skill.

" Their timing was off," Karin called to Mindy.

The ball was in play again, coming this time to the Rockridge side and passing from forward to forward. Carla got in the clear and heaved one of her mighty shoulder shots. It was spectacular and daring, and it looked for a second as if it might be good, but the ball grazed the rim and dropped off. Mindy, not ready for Carla's shot, was slow on the rebound and lost it. A five-foot-ten guard covering Mindy got possession. The ball went from guard to guard, weaving back into Grandville territory. Karin had no time to bemoan the swiftness with which the ball had left the Rockridge half of the court. The Grandville forwards had it and with that lightning pass they had used on the first play landed another basket.

Grandville 4, Rockridge 0.

The spectators went wild. Grandville rooters thundered their approval. The clackety clack of a cheer rent the vast gymnasium. Its rhythm swelled, but groans sailed out from the Rockridge fans. " Get with it, Rockridge. Get with it! "

Carla called time out.

This unusual tactic, so early in the first quarter, brought a howl of surprise from the Rockridge stands. " Where's the coach? Whatcha calling time out for so soon? Where's Fletcher? "

The team huddled in a circle. Carla, breathing hard, spoke in gasps. " They're playing a rough game."

" We know that," Liz snapped. " What are we going to do about it? "

" Play their own game," Carla panted.

" Miss Fletcher wouldn't approve," Mindy cut in.

Liz answered before Carla could reply. " Miss Fletcher's up in the stands, looking down. She left us to play this game on our own."

" What do you think, Karin? " Carla looked distraught. " You're our best shot. Do you back me on this? "

Karin took her time answering. She didn't know what to say. Mindy was right — Miss Fletcher would be furious if they met Grandville's rough tactics on their own level. Yet she had to admit Liz was right too — the coach had left them on their own. They had to do something more than they were doing or Grandville would skyrocket them to kingdom come.

" It's up to you. Carla," she said slowly. " You're captain."

What Karin was really thinking was: Look, this is sticky stuff, and I'm staying out of it. You're still fighting that old battle of Bo Jensen versus Miss Fletcher, man coach versus woman. Maybe Miss Fletcher realized that. Maybe that's why she brought this thing to a showdown tonight.

If Carla decided to call the signals for abandoning Miss Fletcher's brainy methods and pitch in with a rougher game, Karin would not like it. But she could understand. Rockridge needed help, needed it badly. They were in a tight spot, having Grandville stampede them like that on the first two plays. It called for drastic measures of defense and offense. Miss Fletcher's methods, without Miss Fletcher to call the signals, were not much use to them.

Someone had to take over, and that logical someone was the captain.

Karin could read the worry signals in Carla's face, the responsibility and indecision.

" O. K.," she said, " we haven't any choice. We'll play this game the way Bo Jensen would have played it."

" The way Bo Jensen would have played it! " Mindy sounded shocked.

" Yes," Carla's voice, once she had made up her mind, took on the ring of confidence. " Get back in and give it everything you've got."

The girls came out of the huddle. As the whistle called them back to the game, Carla put a detaining hand on Karin's arm. " Skeets, you'll see basketball played as you never have before, and you'll be in it up to your neck."

" I never played this kind of game," she said.

" Don't worry. You'll catch on. Remember one word, survival. And every time you get that ball in your hands, shoot. Just shoot. Anyway and anyhow you can."

" What about fouls? " Karin asked.

" This game is going to be stepped up so fast that no one's going to know what's happening, not even the referees."

Karin went back to her position. Her throat felt like sandpaper, dry and scratchy. Her hands were moist. She couldn't stand still. She moved around, restless and uneasy.

The whistle blew.

When the ball came over into Rockridge territory, Carla caught it. It went to Karin to Mindy back to Carla. Carla's guard tried to intercept. There was a tangle of flying arms and legs. Carla's guard let out a cry of pain and rubbed her shin, yet Karin, watching closely, saw no sign of body contact, and the whistle did not stop the game. Carla kept the ball in the clear while the limping guard hurled herself after her, too late. Carla's shoulder shot heaved the ball in a neat arc toward the rim. It went in, clean, perfect.

Visitors 4, Rockridge 2.

Rockridge sent up a long, hard cheer.

"We're with it," Carla shook her hands over her head toward her guards. "Send them to us and we'll land them as fast as you slam them over!"

The ball went from the referee to the Grandville forward. She caught it and sent it to another forward. Liz, covering her, did everything but twist her arm. Karin, watching, drew in a sharp gasp of surprise. The Grandville forward broke away, pivoted, heaved the ball toward the basket hanger. Sue forced the shorter girl to get rid of it and the ball went back to the first forward, then back to Sue's forward, then out to the girl Deedie was guarding. It weaved back and forth, each time the Rockridge guard forcing the Grandville forward to get rid of the ball.

Karin had never seen such basketball. It was what Carla had promised, swift, dynamic, tough. The pace was terrific. Karin had all she could do to follow the ball. A half dozen times Karin expected to hear a foul called, yet the action was so swift, no one could tell what was happening.

Liz got the ball at last. She sent it zooming over the heads of the Grandville forwards. Karin, at the mid-line, caught it. Her guard pressed her, trying to stop her shot.

It's shoot right away or never, she thought. Even if the Grandville guards had not been blocking her pass, she would have felt impelled to shoot. Carla had given her orders.

Every time you get your hands on the ball, shoot.

Remember, the word is *survival*.

She let go in a strong hook shot that brought a thunder-

101

ous roar from the stands. Her eye was good, her timing perfect. The ball banked, then dropped through the rim and the netting with a swish.

Visitors 4, Rockridge 4.

One of the Grandville guards had wrenched an ankle on the play and the team called time out. They huddled around their coach at the side line. Karin took her first good look at Skip Hennessy. He was perhaps in his middle forties, but he appeared younger, and he met his girls with the springy gait of an athlete. His bony face looked shrewd.

He seems clever enough to come up with almost anything, Karin thought. I wonder what he'll throw our way next.

She soon found out. In the first play following the time out, it was clear that Grandville had been instructed to switch from a shifting zone to a tight man-to-man defense. The movements of the guards indicated this change. Each guard was now assigned to a specific forward. Karin had drawn the huskiest of the lot. She had no time to conjecture about the disadvantage of this because the game was on again.

The man-to-man strategy of the Grandville guards was the most skillful defense Karin had ever seen. They guarded as closely as the law allowed without body contact. They froze into position over the Rockridge forwards whenever Rockridge tried to pass or shoot. Karin couldn't move without touching her guard. She saw that Mindy and Carla were having the same trouble. This meant that the Grandville forwards on the other side of the court were getting the ball. They got it with alarming regularity and sank it in. The score built up. Fast. The scoreboard clicked off the Grandville baskets. At the end of the first quarter it was Grandville 16, Rockridge 4.

Five of the Grandville points had been made at the foul

102

line, with Karin the worst offender, having one personal and two technical fouls against her already.

Carla knelt beside Karin during the quarter break. "What's wrong, Skeets?"

"I'm not used to this kind of game. When we played it Miss Fletcher's way, we played it cagey and brainy, and we licked them. I've never practiced this powerhouse stuff."

"Then take it a little easier."

"You said to shoot every time I got the ball. Anyway, anyhow. I've got a healthy pair of arms and legs. Everytime I try to use them that guard of mine tangles me up. I can't seem to shoot without fouling. Maybe you'd better take me out and put Babs in."

"No, we can't afford to lose you. Not against Grandville. You're our best shot. What you need to do is calm down and not let that big guard scare you. You're too excited. Take it easy, Skeets."

"Maybe we all ought to do that, Carla," Mindy chimed in. "Maybe we ought to forget the Bo Jensen stuff and do what Miss Fletcher taught us to do."

Carla's face was set. "We don't dare change back now. If we let up on this all-out game we're playing, they'll pile up fifty points before the half is over."

"But this way we're fouling all over the lot," Mindy insisted.

"It's better than letting them run away with us," Carla was adamant. "At least we're holding them some. Their man-to-man defense is costing them something too. It keeps us from shooting, but it sure tires those Grandville guards out fast. They'll be running through their guard line-up in no time."

"I've got news for you," Karin said dryly, as they got back to the game. "That husky one guarding me is immortal. She was frozen in the ice of Tibet."

"Stay away from her," Carla said.

"What do you mean, stay away from her? Wherever I go, she gets there first."

"Then keep your hands off her."

If the first quarter was tough, the second was a shambles. Rockridge had the center throw. Carla took it, heaved it to Mindy who sent it to Karin. Karin leaped for it. The palms of her hands ached from the impact. She shifted, dribbled, feinted a throw toward Carla.

"Shoot!" the crowd screamed. "Skeets, shoot!"

She bounced the ball once, trying to duck under the guard's arm but the girl shifted and stopped her. She drew back, holding the ball for a shot. In another second the whistle would blast her ear off for holding.

She had to get rid of it. Carla was too far away, Mindy was covered. It was shoot or nothing. She let go, a tremendous shot that banked against the backboard and plopped into the basket. Applause, whistles, cheers. The referee's whistle pierced the shouts. "Charging. Berglund," she called.

"I never touched her!" Karin was sure she hadn't.

"You sure did." The guard snapped back. "You pelted that ball clear into my solar plexus."

The referee beckoned to Karin. An official warning. "Berglund. One more foul and you're out."

Karin kept her head down as the Grandville forward stepped up to the foul line. She dropped the ball in.

Grandville 17, Rockridge 4.

The ball was in play and Liz Ekstrom got it. She worked it across the Grandville side by clever pass work until she brought it to the mid-line. Liz sent it to Carla who passed to Karin. Karin tossed it to Mindy near the basket. It was doubtful that Mindy could sink it with her guard bearing down on her, but if Mindy passed it back to Karin, Karin might, if she were near enough, tap it in.

Karin signaled Mindy. Mindy feinted a shot, then passed under her guard's arm. Karin caught it. She pivoted, bounced behind her, held the ball to the side. She was close enough for a shot. She decided to pivot, dribble, then with her back to the basket try for a surprise over-head shot.

It was risky and tricky. It took steady hands.

She pivoted away from her guard, dribbled, then with a swift thrust let the ball sail back over her head at the basket. It skimmed along the rim and dropped off. Mindy got the rebound and tried for a basket. It wavered on the rim.

Now, she thought, now for a tip-in.

She reached up and her arm sawed the air, hacking the Grandville guard. The whistle stopped the game.

"Personal foul. Berglund."

The next few moments went by in a blur for Karin. She saw the heads of the officials bent together, heard the shouts from the stands. Light and sound pressed against her, overhead glare, the babel of spectators. In her mouth, the bitter taste of personal failure.

I'm out, she thought. They're yanking me out.

Then the walk off the court to the bench. Shame and frustration and relief. Relief to be out of that ordeal once and for all.

She watched Babs go in for her, watched her charge across the court, watched her pile up the fouls even faster than Karin had done. She did not last through the second quarter. Neither did Liz. In her desperate efforts to get that ball across the mid-line, she was called for holding, pushing, even tripping. She went out just before the buzzer ended the second quarter.

105

Karin took a quick look at the score as she got up to join her teammates for the intermission. It read Grandville 26, Rockridge 13.

It was a chastened team that gathered in the Rockridge headquarters during the intermission. Babs looked sullen, Liz looked as if she had been crying. Deedie, Sue, Carla, and Mindy, those who had stayed with the mess during the entire half, were on the point of exhaustion.

When the door opened and Miss Fletcher stood framed in the opening, Karin thought the girls would run and fling their arms around her.

Mindy spoke for them all. " I was never so glad to see anyone," she said.

They gathered around the coach. She went straight to the point, wasting neither time nor words. " Now we start all over again," she began. " Those who are left in the game will have to forget how tired they are. You'll have to go out there and do your best with the time that's left."

"Will you tell us what to do, Miss Fletcher? " Carla asked. " I think we're all ready to listen."

" We'll start with the figure-eight attack. Follow the floor patterns outlined on the board. No roughhouse, no over-guarding. You, Carla, watch that especially. Don't play spectacular. Play smart. You don't need that kind of stuff if you play the way you've been taught. With proper ball-handling and sure timing."

She glanced from one to the other of those tired faces. Karin could see the coach's mouth soften, the flash of sympathy in her eyes.

" I'll put in the best substitutes we've got to replace the girls who were fouled out. You'll be a crippled team, but the game isn't over. You're not a beaten team. You still can win. Go in there and do the best you can."

The warning buzzer called them back to the gym.

Karin sat on the benches and watched Rockridge try for a comeback. The going wasn't easy. They were tired, dog-tired, but they stayed with it. They played it Miss Fletcher's way this time, Carla and Ellie Thompson covering the court, Mindy staying close to the basket for short shots and rebounds.

Rockridge was fighting now. The girls were giving it everything they had. They began to score, to score heavily. Grandville, tired from their man-to-man defense, began to foul. The Rockridge score piled up.

At the end of the third quarter it was Grandville 37, Rockridge 34.

Miss Fletcher stayed with them this time, directing the new offensive. She sent in substitutes with instructions. She called time out when necessary. The girls, tired though they were, followed her orders to the hilt. One thing was clear. The hours of repetitious drilling were standing Rockridge in good stead. They were pounding out their plays with deadly precision, getting the ball, keeping it, sinking the shots.

Grandville's game began to go to pieces under the battering attack. They pushed the panic button. Their footwork became sloppy, their timing was gone.

The stands behind Karin were screaming their heads off for Rockridge to stay with it, to keep the ball and win the game. Rockridge did. When the final buzzer rasped across the court Karin glanced up at the scoreboard.

It read Visitors 46, Rockridge 52.

It had been close but they had made it. Miss Fletcher had pulled her team together for a surprising and decisive success.

CHAPTER 12

IF STEVE had anything to say about the Grand-ville game, he was not saying it to Karin. During the rest of that week she hardly laid eyes on him. They had never been chummy at school, and Karin was not invited by his sister to go over to the Fletcher barn for special coaching.

There might have been several reasons for this. For one thing, Miss Fletcher was a lot busier than usual, straighten-ing out the mess of the Grandville game. She ran back and forth between the superintendent's and the principal's offices. She had interviews with Karin's grandfather and other members of the recreation committee. She talked to the press. In fact, she was under so much pressure from so many sources that basketball practice was postponed for several days.

Thus Karin had no way of knowing the effect on her relationship with Miss Fletcher of that damaging scene before the Grandville game. She worried about it a good deal. Several times she was on the verge of going to the coach. She would get as far as Miss Fletcher's office and then either lose her nerve or discover that the coach was not in.

Steve did not call Karin up. This was unprecedented, for, while he shied away at school, he had never let two days go by without getting in touch with her. Even more un-usual was Steve's silence around the school building. Out-spoken to a fault, especially about girls basketball, Steve was expected to say plenty about the Grandville game.

But it was a silent Steve Fletcher who made his way through the halls of Rockridge High School, looking neither to the right nor the left, his mouth set in a non-committal line.

108

He's playing the fox, Karin thought. His sister is on pretty thin ice, leaving her team to go it alone for half that game. Steve probably knows that if he does his usual sounding off, it might hurt his sister right now.

If Steve was being unusually silent, there were plenty of people who were not. Despite her drastic action in leaving her team, Miss Fletcher's girls had won. And they had won because she came back into the game. It had been a calculated risk, but the coach had shown how right she was. She had scored her point. So many who had openly criticized her appointment and methods now came over to her side. She suddenly had more supporters than enemies.

Sean Daly became one of the stanchest supporters. Under the headline *Vindication of a Coach*, he wrote in his column, "It was a real cocky team, supercharged with self-confidence, that needled its coach into retreating to the bleachers during the first half of the Rockridge–Grandville game."

Then he went on: "Behind the team is a community that has never given this woman coach an even break. Now maybe both the team and the town will give Miss Fletcher that even break. She certainly earned it the other night."

"Sean Daly's a fine one to be talking about our supercharged self-confidence," Mindy said hotly as she clipped out his article and pasted it in her scrapbook. They were at Mindy's house, in her room, holding a post mortem on that hectic game.

Mindy snorted. "Sean Daly handworked the pump that inflated our egos. Right in his column he said we'd win for sure. Now he's blaming the cockiness on us. Just like a man, the old turncoat."

Karin was not too concerned about anything Sean Daly said, either before or after the game. What bothered her

109

was her own part in that tumultuous evening.

She had a lot to think about, even without the action photographs that accompanied Sean Daly's account staring up at her. A dozen shots taken at the game were spread across the lower portion of the page. Two of them featured Karin. In one she was making an attempted hook shot at the basket. The picture showed her fouling, as her arm hit the guard. The caption was, " Skeets Berglund tries one of her famous shots and fouls."

The second photograph showed her walking to the bench, her head down, her features barely visible. The caption read, " Skeets Berglund fouled out early in game because she played too rough."

Mindy snatched the paper away. " Here, give me that. Don't beat yourself on the head on account of those pictures, Skeets. It wasn't your fault. Carla called the signals for a high-geared game and you followed orders. Besides, it isn't true that you played rough. You just never learned how to play that kind of game. No wonder you fouled out so soon. You've got nothing to be ashamed of, Skeets."

Shame was part of Karin's mixed emotions but the smallest part, really. It was humiliating to walk through the school building and see schoolmates look at you, slantwise, as much as to say, What happened to *you* in the Grandville game?

But she had bigger worries than that. She still had no idea how much ground she had lost with Miss Fletcher. It had been Karin's song about the coach's pet expression that had acted as the tinderbox to the pre-game explosion. It had not yet been explained. The time, the opportunity, and the courage had eluded Karin whenever she felt impelled to set things right.

Then there was her grandfather. His temper seemed very short whenever he talked to her these days. Of course

110

he was almost as busy as Miss Fletcher trying to straighten out what had happened at the Grandville game. He questioned Karin about it, the scene in the office, the attitude of the girls, the trouble over techniques and methods, Carla's decision to play a high-powered game, everything and anything, until Karin wanted to clap her hands over her ears and scream, " Oh, for heaven's sake, let me alone, please! "

He did not scold Karin for being fouled out. It might have been easier for her if he had! He merely harped on what a pity it was that the team had made that great comeback without her. She knew what he was thinking, without his having to say it. The Grandville victory had been a bittersweet one for him. True, it was a feather in his cap, a personal triumph, because it proved he had picked a coach who could use her head. But his granddaughter had let him down. The granddaughter, of whom he was so proud, had fouled out.

He never said these things, and maybe he did not even think them, but Karin felt that he was thinking them. This was even worse than an open squabble between them. She had been growing increasingly fond of her grandfather, and now this had happened. If it did not spoil their closeness, it served at least to create a strain between them, a problem unaired and unsolved.

Moreover, the whole unpalatable mess took the edge off basketball for her, temporarily at least. She had been coming to love the sport, to get a tremendous bang out of it. It was not the answer to all her adjustments in this new and strange environment, but it helped. It had helped a lot.

It had given her something to strive for, not just alone, but with others, and that brought the filling of a great need. The need to belong and to have something to give.

She had never wanted to be the most popular girl in the school, but she was not like Steve either, able to go it alone, so to speak. She needed people. She wanted people. She needed the comfort of the group, the feeling of being wanted and approved. She needed to be so good in something that people would come running to her and clap her on the shoulder and say, " Skeets, you were swell last night." Not because she wanted to be a big wheel, but because, frankly, within herself she was still a little insecure, uncertain.

They did not run up to her after the Grandville game. Her schoolmates were friendly, and they still liked her, but she felt they were watching with a curiosity that said: " Well, Skeets Berglund, where do you go from here? Which way is the cat going to jump next? "

She carried the burden around inside her for the rest of the week and might have forever if she had not had a date with Eric on Friday night.

He was especially gentle with her that evening, seeming to understand that she had something on her mind and didn't feel like talking as much as usual. He gave her the " red-carpet treatment," as she called it, bringing her a corsage of red roses to pin on her beaver coat and taking her to dinner at the best restaurant in Rockridge, The Blue Willow, where there were music and candles and white-linen tablecloths. He even ordered a shrimp cocktail for her, without her asking, because it was one of her favorites. Then he drove her all the way over to Prairie City because the movie was one she had been talking about for weeks. He held her hand through the movie, pressing it from time to time, as much as to say, " Whatever's bothering you, Skeets, I'm with you all the way."

She wouldn't have spoiled the evening for the world by talking about her troubles, but it was Eric who forced it

112

out of her. They were in the kitchen having the snack her grandmother had left for them. He set down his cup and said, " Skeets, why don't you just spit the whole thing out to your Swedish-uncle Eric? "

" It's nothing. Honestly, it's nothing, Eric."

" It's big enough to make a clam out of you all evening and make you leave half your shrimp cocktail and slump down in your seat through the most exciting movie we've seen since you invaded the wide-open spaces. And you want me to believe it's nothing? "

" I'm just tired, I guess. Gramp's birthday is coming along soon, and you know what that means! The whole house has been turned upside down already getting ready for his party."

He looked at her, long and hard, with that special gentleness in his glance that was just Eric.

" Skeets, don't try to kid me. It isn't Gramp's birthday party. It's you."

She shuffled around the things on the table before she answered, rearranging the sugar bowl and the salt and pepper shakers and the napkin holder.

" Eric, I'm homesick." He reached over and put his hand over hers and this action, so spontaneous and kind, unleashed the flood inside.

" I want my father, Eric. I need to talk to him. Things seem suddenly all wrong. I don't know what to do next."

Eric took out his reading glasses from his pocket and slipped them on. He mussed up his hair, pulling it over his forehead in a cowlick. He tried to assume a stern expression, puckering his mouth and putting creases between his eyes.

" Now, daughter," he said, " tell me what's on your mind."

He looked so comical, she burst out laughing, then

113

clapped her hand over her mouth and softened the noise.

"Sh," she said, "you'll wake up the house."

"*I'll* wake up the house. But anyway, I'm glad to hear you laughing again." When he was getting ready to leave, he said, "Skeets, you won't talk and maybe I shouldn't make it my business, but I think I know what's bothering you, and I think I know the answer."

"What?"

He slipped his woolen muffler inside his coat collar. "Why don't you go in and see Miss Fletcher, have a talk with her?"

"I'm afraid she'll blast my ears off."

"You may be surprised at what she'll say and do. Besides, wouldn't it be better to have your ears blasted off than to eat your heart out like this?"

"I suppose so," she said. "But something else is on my mind. Something about you and me." She took the corsage off her coat and held it in her hand while she talked to him.

"Yes?"

"You've been swell to me, Eric, and you're the last person whose feelings I'd want to hurt." She paused. "It's about Gramp's birthday party. Three weeks ago I asked Steve. Now I'm not so sure I did the right thing, with this Grandville game mess and Steve so quiet and all. But I did ask him, Eric. I hope you won't be angry."

He leaned down and kissed her on the cheek and then whispered close to her ear. "I'd rather be with you than any girl I know. You're a lot of fun, Skeets. And I was crazy about you from that first day when you stood in our kitchen and said, 'I should think you'd hate it to have a girl thrown at you.'"

He touched her cheek lightly. "But I don't kid myself, Skeets. I know the score."

114

She held on to the sleeve of his topcoat, unwilling to let him go. Suddenly Eric seemed the one sure thing in her life, the one person who did not change.

"It's because Gramp pushed us together," she said lamely, looking for excuses for her attitude. "I wish he wouldn't. Then maybe we could relax, and I wouldn't be so perverse."

He winked at her, a long, slow wink that screwed up the left side of his face. "It isn't perverseness that makes you want Steve, Skeets. You can fool some of the people all of the time but not your Swedish-uncle Eric. You're as crazy about that guy as I am about you."

CHAPTER | 13

KARIN WENT to see Miss Fletcher in her office bright and early that Monday morning. It was one of the most difficult things she had ever had to do. She walked up and down the corridor of the physical education ell a half dozen times before she got up the courage to knock on the door.

"Come in," the coach's voice rang out. "Oh, Karin, it's you." The tone may have been exactly what it had always been, warm and friendly, but Karin was too nervous to tell. "Sit down."

"No, thanks. I mean, I'm in a hurry, sort of. I have a class in five minutes." Miss Fletcher nodded. Karin had prepared several elaborate speeches but now, confronted by Miss Fetcher, she forgot them all and blurted out the thing uppermost in her mind. "I'm sorry," she said. "I don't know how to tell you how really sorry I am, Miss Fletcher."

The coach got up and came around to Karin. She stood next to her. "Would it make you feel better if you told me the truth about that song?" she asked. "I'd like to hear your version."

Karin nodded, gulping, reaching for words that would clarify the incident. "Well, to begin, it was all in fun, you understand. I don't mean making fun of you," she added quickly. "Just among ourselves. A kind of safety valve after those hard practice games. We'd be worn out and glad to be finished and — "

"And my coaching methods were exhausting," Miss Fletcher said with the trace of a twinkle in her eye.

"Yes. No, I mean they weren't exactly exhausting, but we had to let off steam once the practice was over. It could have been anything, you understand. Mindy's nosiness or Carla's temper or Babs's clumsiness or the hard time I have making up my mind about things."

"So you chose the coach's crazy vocabulary because she wasn't there."

"No, no! It's not that we thought it was crazy. We'd just heard it so often and — " Karin stopped. "The more I open my big mouth, the more I put my foot in it. Maybe I would have done better if I hadn't tried to explain."

"No, I'm glad you came in, Karin. You did the right thing. It's all past now, water over the dam, and I'm willing to forget it if you are."

"Then you weren't mad at me, Miss Fletcher?"

Miss Fletcher studied the pamphlets and papers on her desk before she answered. "I wouldn't be telling the truth if I said I wasn't angry. I was, intensely so, for the time being. I didn't relish the idea of having the girls I liked so much poke fun at me when I wasn't around." Karin looked away. "But then I remembered that once upon a time I had had a teacher of whom I was very fond, a math

116

teacher. She understood children and we all loved her, but she did some funny things, like kicking off her shoes under the desk when she thought we didn't see her and putting her finger between her teeth when she was thoughtful and she had a pet expression. 'Remember, girls and boys, it's stick-to-itiveness that counts in life.'"

Karin glanced back at her.

"If we heard that once, Karin," she said, "we heard it a thousand times before that year was up." She put her hand on Karin's shoulder. "All is forgiven," she said, "come down to practice this afternoon and we'll make up for lost time." Then as Karin was turning to leave the office, she added, "By the way, you'd better stop by at the barn some night soon." She hesitated. "Steve says he wants to get on with your portrait."

Karin went through that day with flying colors. She got ninety-five in an English quiz, she found the lost turtle in the science lab, she gave a history recitation that made Eric, walking out of class with her, comment, "Hey, you, what are you planning to do, run for the Senate or something?" She even got through her math problem without help.

In the gym that afternoon, there was a new atmosphere that Karin summed up in one word, "Willingness." The team listened carefully. They tossed off their boredom and impatience. They even asked questions.

"Boiling it down," Miss Fletcher said at the end of a long analysis, "what I'm trying to do is to train you to make split-second decisions on the court. That's the reason for all these drills. I want you to learn how to position your bodies for any court situation even before you receive the ball."

"Will you please explain the advantage of that?" Carla was the spokesman for her team.

117

"If you know which way you're going to throw that ball before you get it, it will eliminate body contact. It makes for fluid floor movement that's very efficient. This is the difference between a mediocre and a superior team."

Their practices, oddly enough, became less boring once they stopped fighting the coach and entered into the spirit of what she was trying to do with and for them. With the sharp lesson of the Grandville game behind them, they were willing to work harder, without grumbling or antagonism.

The Rockridge coach took her now co-operative team into the tightening competition of the county tournament. They beat Prairie City and Samson again, on the home courts of these teams, with scores of 51–39 and 43–21. They went down the line of county tournament entries with a fresh outburst of enthusiasm and energy.

At Leadville they had a close call, 35–32. They met Wilmington and Holbrook on the Rockridge court and lost to the former on an off day when Carla and Sue and Mindy were all home with colds, but they clobbered Holbrook, still without Carla, 60–33.

While Carla was absent, the girls elected Karin substitute captain. This pleased her, not just because of the implied popularity, but because it showed that in spite of the Grandville game, the girls still had faith in her. On the whole things were brighter than they had been that night when she had wept on Eric's sympathetic shoulder. Then along came her grandfather's birthday party.

The day dawned brilliant and clear, a sparkling winter day. Karin chuckled to herself as she looked out upon the sweep of farmland, with its crust of frost and faint patches of snow left from the last storm.

"Knowing Gramp, one might almost think he'd put in his order with the weather bureau."

118

All day the big house teemed with preparations for the party. It would be a big one, as Ed Berglund's parties always were, with as many people invited as they could crowd into the house. The rooms were full of strange sights and sounds and good smells. Farmhands stamped in the back way, hurling their heavy boots on the floor, tearing off their jackets. Then, in shirt sleeves and stocking feet, they moved the furniture from the living room, cleared the floor for dancing, waxed and polished it.

Karin, in old slacks and a shabby sweater salvaged from her New England days, was in the middle of everything.

By six o'clock the big house had cleared of people. The table was set in blue and yellow for the *smörgasbord*. The two giant refrigerators had slammed on the last batch of food, prepared and waiting to be reheated before serving. The last resounding smack of the hammer had faded into silence. Boots and jackets, coats and parkas had disappeared from the lower hall almost as quickly as they had piled up.

The house lay quiet, with almost a brooding silence before the inrush of guests, the thumping of drums and piano keys, the wailing of saxophone and trumpet would liven it up again.

Now Karin had the big house to herself. She wandered from room to room, looking into the empty kitchen, with hardly a trace of this afternoon's bustle; in her grandfather's office, his incoming and outgoing letter baskets were arranged neatly on his desk, his chair swung outward as if he had just jumped from it to rush off on an errand.

She went through the smaller sitting room to the large one, which, stripped of so much of its finery, bare save for a few chairs along the wall and the crystal and cranberry lamps, looked as if the family had moved out.

The house no longer overwhelmed her as it had the first

night she had stepped into it. She understood this house now, its size and its ostentation, even as she had grown to understand somewhat better the grandfather who had furnished it.

Tonight was his birthday celebration and she wanted it to be especially happy for him, partly to heal the breach of the Grandville game, but mostly because she liked to please him. He was almost like a child in his gratitude when anyone did something nice for him.

She had taken special pains to help with the decorations. And upstairs in her closet, hidden safely at the back was the one gift she knew would please him most. It was a photograph of the two of them together on their horses, she on Ebony, her grandfather on his favorite stallion, Demon. Oscar had snapped them one day, in color, and Karin had ordered an enlargement as a surprise. Framed in silver, it made a handsome gift, and her grandfather would love it. " It shows how much you are like him," Oscar had said, looking at the enlargement. " The same nose and good bones and wide smile. The same blue eyes with the same look. And see, even the way you sit on your horses, with your backs so straight, your heads so high, your hands just so. Yah, he will like this."

Karin went upstairs to her bedroom. When she opened the door, the fragrance of her favorite perfume touched her nostrils. Mamie. Mamie had been in to get out Karin's dress for this evening and be sure it was pressed, and Mamie never lost a chance to spray herself with Karin's perfume. She smiled. Well, let her, what harm.

She took a quick shower and put on her underthings and crinolines. Then she turned to the old satinwood clothes stand on which hung the dress she would wear tonight.

With great care she slipped it over her head and fas-

120

tened it. She turned to look at herself in the full-length mirror.

The dress was red satin, with a scoop neckline and a voluminous skirt, which made her small waistline appear waspish. The color made her hair seem even blonder than it was, and her skin, translucent.

"My dear," her grandmother had said when they bought the dress, especially for this occasion, "I had such a dress once. It was almost the same color as this, and I kept it long after I could no longer wear it, calling it my dress of a lifetime because I never again had a dress that I loved so much, not even my wedding dress."

Karin now thought how truly her grandmother had voiced Karin's own sentiments toward this dress. "It makes me feel beautiful," she said to her reflection in the mirror.

In the hollow of her throat she hung a lavalier. "Here, Karin," her grandmother had said. "This is no longer becoming to me. It pleases me to know you will wear it." It was simply designed, a diamond surrounded by garnets and pearls and there were earrings to match. She wondered if Steve would like the way she looked tonight. She had selected this dress for him, really, because it was his favorite color. Tonight Steve would lead the march with her, the "birthday march" when her grandfather stood at the head of the room and his household and guests lined up to shake his hand and wish him many happy returns of the day.

Karin had fought for the right to have Steve by her side at that moment. Her grandfather had been put out that she hadn't picked Eric for the honor.

"He's the son of my best friend, Karin. It would please me to have Eric with you, to look down that room and see you on his arm."

"But I've already asked Steve to be my partner for this

121

party, Gramp. I can't change that now. Eric understands, and I wish you'd try to understand too."

So she had won. It would be Steve.

She wanted Steve here by her side tonight for several reasons, and one of them was to silence people like Liz Ekstrom who believed he did not really care for Karin but kept her friendship because she was useful to him.

There was a light tap on her door.

" Yes? " she called.

" You're wanted on the telephone, Karin."

" All right, Mamie. I'll take it in the upstairs den."

This was a small combination sitting and music room with television and a record player and stacks of books. She opened her door, nodded to Mamie who hurried toward her own quarters while Karin turned the other way toward the den. Her wide skirt and crinolines rustled as she walked toward the telephone. She hardly dared sit down in this dress.

" Hello."

" Hello, Karin? "

" Hi, Steve! "

A long, long pause. "Karin, I can't make it tonight. I just can't."

" You can't make it? " The words were halting, her own voice sharp with incredulity.

" No, I can't. I'm working. Up to my neck in paint, covered with the stuff. It would take me two hours to get it off."

" Come late then."

" No, I'm in the middle of something. I want to finish it."

" But, Steve, this isn't just any party. This is my grandfather's birthday. This is big."

" I can't help it, Karin."

She paused, drawing in a deep breath. Outrage almost

122

choked her but she forced the words out. " I want you here tonight, Steve, late if necessary, but under no circumstances must you stand me up tonight. This is important. It's a must."

" It's no use arguing. I've made up my mind." She didn't answer. " Do you hear me, Karin? Are you there? " She heard him click the telephone. " Karin, are you there? "

Slowly she set the telephone in its cradle. She stared at it. So this was Steve. He meant what he said. It would have been futile to argue with him over the telephone.

She walked out into the hall. The grandfather clock standing in the corner told her that it would be a good hour before the first guests arrived.

I'll go to him, she thought. Perhaps I can persuade him how important tonight is to me. No, not Steve, once he makes up his mind, no one can move him. . . . But I've got to. I've got to bring him here tonight. If he doesn't come to my grandfather's birthday party, it's as if he had rejected me publicly. There could never be any future for me and Steve even as friends here in Rockridge, not after everyone expects him to lead the birthday march with me.

Her pride rebelled against going to Steve, but she flung that off. This was no time for pride. This was a time for action, the most drastic action she could summon. She ran to her room and snatched the first coat she could lay her hands on. It happened to be the black and white check, which she had worn on her trip from Connecticut. She flung it over her shoulders, shrugging into it, not closing it because if she tried it would spoil her beautiful dress.

Fortunately both her grandparents were in their rooms, dressing. The house seemed desolate, empty. She ran down the stairs, gripping the banister, almost catching her heel on one of the treads. Out fast, the back way, watch your step. There's some ice around even on the cleared paths.

Wait, easy does it. Who's that skulking in the shadows of the barn? It's no one skulking, it's Oscar! Oscar finishing his chores in the stables.

He swung toward her, turning his powerful flashlight upon her face. She blinked, blinded, turned away. "It's me, Ozzie."

"Karin! What you doing out here this time of night? They forgot something for the party?"

"No, Ozzie. Not that. It's something else." She might as well tell him, take him into her confidence. Oscar was one person she could trust. "It's Steve, Ozzie. He says he won't come over tonight."

"Ah, that is not good. That is not at all good."

"I'm going after him. I'm going to bring him here."

He came toward her, holding out a detaining hand. "Karin, wait. No, you must not do that."

She was halfway into the sedan. "Why not?"

He dropped his hand. "I do not know why. Just that I feel it is not good."

She turned on the ignition and started the engine. Oscar was at the door, holding it open. "I go with you, yah."

"No. Thanks just the same, Ozzie. This is one thing I've got to do alone."

"Maybe so. Maybe so. But you be careful, Karin. Yah, take care. He has a quick temper, that boy."

She leaned over to close the door. "I'll be careful."

She drove fast, keeping her eyes strained ahead of her on the straight ribbon of road. No hills, no curves, just miles and miles of road with dirty snow banked along it, stretching back over fields. An occasional farmhouse with its sharp rise of silos whirred by. Naked trees, the hard bright moon, high and distant. Thin shadows on the road. A scurrying rabbit or cat. Otherwise, darkness and silence. Nothing but her own thoughts to keep her company.

124

They were hardly thoughts at all. More like confused squirrels chasing one another in that cage called her brain. No sense to any of it. Fear, mostly, devastating fear that she might fail in her mission, that no matter what she said Steve might not come back with her. He could do that, could refuse her, with finality. She knew it better than anyone.

The car bounced to a stop as she turned in at the Fletcher place. She jumped out, leaving the car door wide open. Slipping and sliding over the icy path, she made her way toward the door of the barn, holding her skirts high. Her eyes searched the upper story of the barn. There were lights, many of them, blazing in the dark night. Steve was there.

Throwing open the door, she flung herself into the barn. The downstairs was pitch black, but she could have found her way across the basketball court in the dark. Once she almost tripped over a mattress someone had left on the floor, but she braced herself against the wall in time. Now, up the stairs, sideways is best, because this dress is so full. Stop, pause a moment now to think, to take a deep breath, to try if possible to still some of this fear.

No, it's no use. I shall have to face him like this, unnerved and unpoised. I cannot do it any other way.

She knocked and then before Steve could answer, she pulled open the door. Steve heard her and turned around. He was wearing the blue dungarees and an old sweater in which he liked to paint. When he had told her that he was covered with paint he had told the truth. His bare arms and hands were full of it. His dungarees were spattered. Some had even splashed on his face. His dark hair, disheveled and stringy, hung over his forehead. He had a half dozen brushes in his hands.

"Karin!"

"Hello, Steve."

"Look out, you'll get this stuff on you." He set down his brushes and wiped his hands.

"Steve, I want you to come back with me. I need you tonight. You've got to be there." He shook his head, slowly wiping the paint from his fingers. "Steve, please."

"Why does this mean so much to you?"

"Can't you understand? It's my grandfather's birthday. I've told everyone you'd be there. We're to lead the birthday march. What will it look like if you don't show up?"

"You worry too much about what people think. Let them think what they want to." He went on with that maddeningly careful job he was doing wiping his fingers one by one. It galled her to see him take it with such insouciance when she was seething.

"Steve, can't you just this once think of someone besides yourself?"

He looked up. "You think I'm selfish."

No, she thought, this is all wrong. This is the exactly wrong approach to get a boy to do anything; even a more docile boy than Steve would rebel at this kind of talk.

She changed her tactics. "I'm sorry I said that. I didn't mean it the way it tumbled out. I'm upset, and bothered. The party won't be complete without you, Steve. Everyone likes your jam sessions. No one in the crowd can pound out jazz on a piano quite the way you can. Once you're there, you always manage to have a good time. In fact, you're the life of the party. You know that's true."

He smiled at her, but it was a strange, aloof smile with no warmth in it. "There's no use appealing to my better nature, Karin. You know I haven't any."

It was meant to be witty, perhaps, in Steve's caustic way. He had said this sort of thing many times before and Karin had let it pass, but tonight she could not throw it off so

126

easily. The remark stung. She rose to the bait.

"Steve," she began, and she was going to say, Steve, I wish you wouldn't talk like that, not tonight, but she stopped short with his name. Because behind him she saw something that gripped her attention. There, uncovered, stood the portrait he was doing of her. "Steve," she exclaimed, "it's finished! You've finished my portrait."

He turned quickly, reaching for the covering, but it was too late. She was past him walking toward the painting.

"Don't touch it!" his voice was sharp. "It's still wet. And it's not finished. You shouldn't look at it."

"I am looking at it," she answered simply. "It's too late now." It was too late indeed. She stood before the canvas standing on its big easel, staring at it. This was her first sight of it, and her instantaneous reaction was shock, quick, sudden dislike of what she saw. At first she could not tell what the matter was. She knew enough about paintings to recognize how nearly done this was and to make allowances for the final touching up, which Steve would do.

Nor had she expected a fine likeness. Steve did not paint that way. But Steve had not caught her at all.

Steve almost spoke her thoughts. "You don't like it." He came over, standing near the picture. "I never promised a likeness."

"It isn't that. I didn't expect a likeness."

"But you admit you don't like it."

"Steve, cover it up. We'll talk about it some other time."

"What's wrong with the painting?" She could see how much her opinion mattered, and she knew she was on very dangerous ground. But Steve was insistent. He stood between her and the door. "I want you to tell me what's wrong with that portrait."

She turned back for another look. "It's cold, for one

127

thing. Cold, cold as ice. No warmth at all. It makes me shiver just to look at it."

"You think because you're an artist's daughter that you know all there is to know about painting."

"You made me tell you what I think of it. Now you're blaming me because it isn't what you wanted to hear."

He turned his back. Well, she thought, there goes my last chance of bringing him back to the party. She started toward the door and he stopped her.

"You've always liked what I did before."

"Yes, Steve, you know that. You know I've always said you had talent, and promise, lots of promise. I can't help it if this portrait disappoints me. We've always told each other the truth. If I lied to you now, you'd know it and you'd hate me for that."

"Why does it disappoint you so much?" he asked. "I can see you liking or not liking something — but disappointment, that's a strong word."

"Because it shows something about you that frightens me, Steve. Something I've tried to overlook or turn away from or tell myself wasn't there. Now I can see it in my own portrait."

"What are you talking about? What have you tried to overlook in me, to turn away from?"

"Coldness, Steve, and self-centeredness. The thing that makes you shy away from social gatherings, from parties like tonight. The thing that makes you do only what you want to do. That keeps you from basketball games. That makes you so changeable and moody and stubborn."

"You're not perfect either," he flared back. "You're pretty much like that domineering grandfather of yours, you know. You needn't talk about me wanting my own way! All you Berglunds are alike, swashbuckling through Greene County as though you owned even the air everybody is breathing."

128

She went over to him. "Steve, let's not quarrel. This is awful, saying these terrible things to each other. Look, I've wanted more than anything to help you. You've got terrific talent. That still stands." She could say things to him she had not been able to say before.

"Steve, you're the last person in the world I'd want to quarrel with." She softened her tone. "Maybe you haven't guessed it, but everyone else has. I'm crazy about you, Steve." She moved toward him, but he stepped back.

He was still angry. "I don't want your love, Karin. It's too possessive, too selfish. You'd always want me to be what you thought I ought to be. Now you want me to paint the way you think I should paint."

"That's not fair, Steve, and you know it."

"Fair? You don't know what the word fair means. You Berglunds sit over there in your big house and expect everyone to run and dance when you whistle. 'Steve, I want you to come to the party tonight, Steve, I want you to do this or do that, to paint my portrait the way I want it.' You're a fine one to talk about selfishness."

She drew back from his vehemence. Her own anger was roused at last, answering his.

"Steve," she said, and her voice had a deadly quiet to it, "when I came here tonight, I wanted very much to take you back to the party. I was even sorry when I saw the portrait and said those things to you. I didn't want to quarrel. But now I don't care. I'm glad we did quarrel. For the first time I can see you as you really are, unfair, unkind, and a little cruel. I don't want you, Steve, for the party or anything else. Good-by."

She turned to go. "Wait!" Steve's voice stopped her. She hesitated, her back toward him, her hand on the door. "This is *my* answer," he flung the words at her, making her turn around. He reached for a knife that lay on the table near the easel. In three deft strokes he slashed the

129

canvas, tearing her portrait to shreds. The strips of canvas hung there, like the long fingers of a dead hand.

She ran down the stairs, across the dark barn, out into the winter night. How she ever covered the distance between the Fletcher barn and her grandfather's house, she she did not know. She drove blindly, seeing nothing. It was Oscar's voice that brought her to her senses.

"Karin, you are back." She hunched over the wheel, sobbing. Oscar did not try to talk to her. He sat beside her, smoothing her hair. She quieted at last, the sobbing left off. She could not tell anyone, not even Oscar, the terrible thing Steve had done to her.

"I'll be all right now," she said. "I'll go in the back door and slip upstairs. I can fix myself up before the guests get here."

In her room she threw off her coat and tossed it on the bed. In the long mirror she saw that her cheeks burned scarlet and that her lipstick was smeared. Her hair was wild about her face. But her dress had survived the stormy scene in Steve's paint-spattered studio without a spot or tear. It looked as fresh as it had when she had slipped into it an hour ago. But it no longer seemed beautiful to her.

"I'll have to wear it tonight," she said aloud, "because I could never explain if I didn't. But I'll never wear it again. Never."

CHAPTER 14

THE QUARREL with Steve shook Karin to her roots. It happened at the worst possible time because the Rockridge team was entering the final games of the county tournament.

She carried the heartbreak within her, unable to talk it out with anyone. It became common knowledge around the school that Karin and Steve had had a squabble. After all, he had stood her up the night of the party. Yet the details of the quarrel remained a mystery. Karin confided in no one, and Steve was the kind who would rather have his tongue cut out than discuss his personal affairs with anyone. Karin had a feeling, unconfirmed of course, that he had not even talked it over with his sister.

Karin, more approachable, was bombarded by questions from well-meaning — and some not so well-meaning — classmates. She had a stock answer for everyone. "Oh, we didn't agree on some important things, that's all."

She got used to raised eyebrows and whispers that suddenly broke off when she stepped into the girls' room or approached a table in the library or cafeteria or banged into the shower room after practice games. Let them talk or think what they wanted as long as they let her alone.

It was not so easy to brush off those close to her. Mindy pumped until she was blue in the face and got nowhere. Eric was willing to listen if Karin wanted to talk, he told her. She kissed him and said: "Eric, you're a real doll. But I wouldn't dump this problem on my worst enemy, much less my best friend. This is one time I've got to struggle through on my own."

Her grandmother worried because she turned down sec-

131

ond helpings for the first time since she'd come out here — and sometimes did not even finish first helpings.

"I don't like the circles under your eyes, Karin," she said. "Are you getting good rest? Maybe you're working too hard, with all that basketball-playing and schoolwork too." Her grandmother, always the soul of tact, avoided mentioning Steve.

Her grandfather, however, thundered what was on his mind. "Karin, this boy isn't worth eating your heart out for. I warned you he had moods. I told you at the start. But now that this quarrel has happened, maybe it's a good thing. You haven't lost anything. So brace up and eat your grandmother's good food and forget him."

Once she was so overwrought by her grandfather's naggings that she jumped up from the table and exclaimed, "Gramp, do you have to preach a sermon at every meal?" Then she ran from the room. Pausing outside the kitchen to control herself, she heard her grandmother say: "Ed, please leave the child alone. Can't you see what she's going through? Let her work it out her own way."

The trouble was that she was not working it out, her own way or anyone else's. Oscar was the most comfort, in his wise, understanding way, because he was the one person who did not search her face these days, looking for signs of bitterness or heartbreak or anger. Yet he was the one who had been closest to her on that eventful night. For he had seen her when she left to go to Steve and he had met her on her return and he had sat with her in silence on that clear winter night and watched her cry her heart out.

Yet Oscar asked no questions. He never mentioned that night. Once or twice she sauntered down to the stables in her loneliness and her grief and to get away from her grandparents, and Oscar let her alone. She wandered down the row of horses, rubbing the nose of a favorite, giving

132

Ebony a lump of sugar, standing and staring at Demon who stamped around his stall or shook his head, whinnying at her.

Only once did Oscar even seem to take note of her unusual silence, her depression over Steve's rejection. They were out riding. The sun went down in a blaze of glory, filling the sky with its dying brilliance.

" It goes down fighting," Oscar said. " But it will come up again tomorrow. Everything in life is like that. Nothing is ever the end."

Nothing is ever the end, she tried to tell herself, repeating Oscar's words again and again, but she did not believe what she said. Clearly this was the end for Steve and her. Why, at school Steve did not even speak to her any more! He did this through the simple expedient of seeing her first and managing to be looking the other way.

So at school, especially, things were very difficult for Karin. She had made up her mind not to talk about it to anyone and she kept resolutely to her decision. Her instincts told her this was the right thing to do. If I hang the story of that quarrel and what I said and Steve said on every dog's tail, it will hurt me a lot more than Steve. For one thing, people don't like a whiner, even when they turn a sympathetic ear. Then if Oscar *is* right the day may come when Steve and I will see things differently; we may make up. So I'm keeping my mouth closed. Then I won't have anything to regret.

It was not easy. All kinds of people seemed eager to have Karin confide in them, including her teachers. It was obvious that something was bothering her, something big and important, for her schoolwork suffered, temporarily at least, as much as her appetite.

If her teachers had scolded her, she thought sometimes that might have been a good thing. It might have waked

133

her out of her apathy. If Mrs. Francis, who could be sarcastic at times, had stood Karin up and lashed into her about that unfinished history assignment, Karin might have been made to snap out of it. She almost longed to hear something like. " *Miss* Berglund, are you making a social visit in this class or do you plan to stay for the rest of the semester? " Several times Mrs. Francis stared at Karin, gave that special sniff that always preceded one of her cutting remarks, then snapped her jaws shut in forbearance.

In math, her weakest subject, she was sure she was doing work below passing. When Mr. Drake asked her to wait after class one day, she thought it was to tell her that unless her work improved she'd have to drop basketball. Instead he went over the most difficult problems with her and gave her a chance to make up the homework for an entire week. As they finished their talk, a twinkle came into his eye and he said, " You know, Karin, there's one equation that I have never learned to solve."

" What's that? " she asked.

" The human equation. Especially girl minus boy equals x. You're a swell girl, Karin, and I admire your stiff upper lip. But don't you let this whatever-it-is get you down inside." His eyes twinkled again. " No man's worth it," he added, " not even me."

Then there was the awful day when during English class she discovered a theme was due and she had completely forgotten it. Miss Matthews asked her to stay after school.

Here it is, Karin thought. This time I'm going to catch it. Mrs. Francis and Mr. Drake are married and they'd make allowances for boy-meets-girl troubles. But not Miss Matthews! I bet she's never even been in love.

So Karin braced herself for a scolding. She could almost

134

forecast, verbatim, Miss Matthews' lecture. "Karin, you've been staring out of the window for a whole week now. Don't you think it's about time you came back to earth? We all have personal problems, but we've got to forget them and face reality and do our job."

This was the way Miss Matthews handled daydreamers.

So Karin almost rolled out of the seat when Miss Matthews began with, "Karin, would you like to talk to me about what's bothering you?"

Karin liked Miss Matthews, liked her salty way of talking, her classroom humor, her strict but fair approach to her students. Of all her teachers, Miss Matthews would have been the one Karin might have opened up to. But she put a bridle on her tongue and turned away with a laconic, "There's nothing to talk about, Miss Matthews."

Miss Matthews watched her in silence for a few moments. Then she said: "Very well, if you won't talk, I'm going to. Karin, I know you and I know Steve, and I like you both."

Karin glanced at her, then away, quickly.

"That's why I want to tell you something. Something that happened to me a long, long time ago. I knew a boy who was much like Steve. Steve paints pictures; this boy wrote stories. We were editors together on the school magazine. So we became very good friends. He would bring me his stories and read them to me, and they were very good for the most part. They showed wonderful promise, a big talent."

Karin glanced back again, and this time she did not look away as Miss Matthews went on.

"One day this boy started a book and he brought it to me when it was half done. And I criticized it, honestly and frankly. I told him the writing was good, but that he hadn't got enough to say yet, not for a book. That it was shallow

135

and had no depth. He was very angry with me, and he took his book and went home and did not speak to me for a long, long time."

Karin wanted to blurt out: Why, that's Steve and me! That's what happened to us, almost exactly what happened. But she ground her teeth, choking back the words.

Miss Matthews went on.

"You may not be interested in what happened to my friend, but I think I'll tell you anyway. He was a fighter pilot in World War II, and he came back in a wheel chair. Then he took up his writing and he had plenty to say, important things." She paused. " I think you might recognize his name if you heard it."

Karin's curiosity overcame her reluctance to talk. " Do you ever see him or hear from him? "

An amused expression filled Miss Matthews' eyes. "Indeed, yes," she said. "He sends me his autograph every Christmas on the handsomest card that decorates my mantel."

Karin got up. She had always enjoyed a friendly relationship with this teacher and she felt safe in saying, " I thought you were going to bawl me out for not doing my theme, Miss Matthews."

"This was a bawling out," Miss Matthews said. "Didn't you recognize it? "

"I — I guess not," Karin stammered.

Miss Matthews walked to the door with her. She said in a voice devoid of her usual schoolmarm's preciseness, a voice suddenly gentle and soft: "What I've been telling you, Karin, is that the male ego is the most tender thing in the world, so we women have all got to learn to handle it gently. Now look, young lady," and her tone reverted all at once to her usual schoolroom treble, "get that paper in to me by Monday." She gave Karin a clap on the shoul-

136

der. Then softly again: "And don't worry your head off wondering how I found out about you and Steve. Nobody told me. I just have a sixth sense about these things."

Karin thought a lot about what Miss Matthews had told her. In a way Miss Matthews had been letting her know that Karin herself was partly responsible for the quarrel with Steve. But more than that, Miss Matthews was telling her that she ought to grow up and learn to be a woman and accept her role as a woman. If she was going to fall in love with a boy like Steve, a boy not easy to handle or understand, she would have to accept the responsibility of getting along with him.

Karin dwelt on these thoughts. She knew that Steve had been wrong, dead wrong, in the way he had talked and acted, but she saw that she had played her part in it too. She wished almost that she might go back and do things all over again.

Steve had said things that shocked her, but they had also made her think. He had accused her of being exactly like her grandfather, of being like the person she knew who most rubbed her the wrong way! Am I really like that? she asked herself. Is there some shred of truth in Steve's accusation that I'm bossy and want to manage people?

It was true enough that she had meddled in Steve's life, wanting to turn him into the best painter she could, wanting always to bring out the talent she knew was there. But it was helpfulness and her fondness for him that had driven her on. She should have let him alone, let him grow and develop in his own way.

It was too late now to change all that. It was too late now for anything but regrets.

Of these she had plenty, and they bothered her, mingling with her frustration over the quarrel with Steve, and hampering her at every turn.

They hampered her most when she stepped out onto the basketball court. She had stopped going over to the Fletcher barn for practice. Her basketball practice was now limited to games with the team at school. Here her problems were difficult and unyielding.

At first she was so upset emotionally that she could not handle the ball. She fumbled and faltered through two games. Miss Fletcher was forced to take her out and send in Ellie Thompson. Gradually, this tension wore off and she regained some of her old control, but then new difficulties set in.

She missed those practice drills at the Fletcher barn. A basketball forward, like a good pianist, was no better than the amount of practice put into the work. Her value to the team had been as a forward who could wham in hard, driving shots from difficult angles that other forwards could not place, and on tip-ins and foul shots. These needed practice, relentless daily practice, which she no longer gave the game.

Added to this was her discomfiture in the presence of Miss Fletcher. Try as she might, Karin could not shake off the nervous feeling that gripped her when the coach was around. It was a strange kind of nervousness, part embarrassment, part mistrust.

This feeling built up. She could not shake it off. She began to imagine all kinds of things about the coach. She felt that Miss Fletcher was constantly watching her or was picking on her, that she had a special tone of voice when addressing Karin, and that she took her out of interschool games where there was no need to do so.

While Karin was going from bad to worse on the courts, the Rockridge team was holding its own. They went through the county tournament, eliminating one opponent after another. They defeated Simonsville twice, 46–37 the

138

first time and with a closer call the second, 39–37. They held Black Rock in the first game 47–44 but lost to them in the second 38–31. However, they went on to defeat West-field by decisive scores of 49–32 and 57–42.

No one was more surprised than the town of Rockridge to hear that their team had come out of the county tourna-ment with number one rating.

Sean Daly gave them a whole column that day, ending his article with: "So the unpredictable Rockridge girls stand in first place in Greene County. This means that they will meet Hanford in the sectional contest, and if they win, go on to the state finals.

"This is a big IF. In the county eliminations, it was touch and go all the way for the girls in hunter green. First they had it, then they didn't. Powerful teams like Red Creek and Grandville showed up the weaknesses in Rock-ridge's game.

"In the Hanford game, Rockridge will meet the strong-est team it has faced to date. Naturally, we would like to see the team from Greene County go to the state finals, but as we said before, it's an awfully big IF."

The week before Rockridge met Hanford in the sec-tional finals was a nightmare for Karin. The team practiced every afternoon, long and hard. These were the practice games to end all practice games! Formerly, there had been a little fun mixed with the tedious routine. Now a grim earnestness hung over the team. Even in the locker room where they liked to blow off steam in jokes and singing, the team maintained its solemn silence. What talk there was, centered around basketball. Too much was at stake.

In addition to this determination to win, another frame of mind pervaded the Rockridge gym. Karin could best describe it as pickiness. Even the best-natured girls felt the strain. They were all under terrific tension. For one thing, their schoolwork had to be given special care, so teachers would not declare them ineligible to play. The basketball players bent over backwards, trying to please classroom teachers with homework and special assignments. Added to this was the daily ordeal of those taut, grueling practices. By the end of that week every girl on the team had a bad case of tournamentitis — nervous fatigue. Tongues lashed out; tempers were short.

The final practice before the Hanford game was a humdinger. Everything that could go wrong — did! Babs plowed her way across the floor bent on destruction. Carla lorded it over the team she captained. Liz found her sneakers that afternoon, hidden in an old wastebasket in the boys' physical education office and she declared publicly to anyone who would listen that Karin had tossed them there.

This final tangle with Liz shattered Karin's already shaken poise. She was completely off her game, highstrung, unable to control her shots.

She had a lot more than Hanford on her mind. She had Steve and rejection and heartbreak.

The varsity was playing the second and third string teams in this practice. Karin, famed for her perfect control at the foul line, was a dud today. Every foul shot she tried teetered and caromed off.

Mindy stood behind Karin, needling her. "Skeets, why don't you let go? You're handling that ball the way you used to. You know better than to grip it like that."

Karin stifled the impulse to box Mindy's ears. She stepped up for another foul shot. This time Mindy said: "Skeets, let go. You know you can't shoot unless you loosen up."

Karin winced. Mindy's meddlesomeness, usually taken in good part, struck a raw nerve.

140

If she needles me once more, Karin thought, best friend or not, I'm going to give her a piece of my mind.

On the next foul shot as Karin moved up to take the ball, Mindy also moved in.

"Skeets, don't grip the ball as if it was glued to your fingers. Let go."

Karin wheeled on Mindy. She bounced the ball at her. "Here, take it yourself, smart aleck."

Mindy jumped back from the ball. It rolled to the side. The two friends faced each other. All the wrath that Karin had stuffed inside these past weeks bubbled to the surface.

"I was only trying to help," Mindy said lamely.

"Help! That's all you're ever trying to do. The trouble is you don't help. You just butt into things that are none of your business. Everybody is sick and tired of your kibitzing, Mindy. Sick and tired of it!"

"Just because you're mad at the world you don't have to take it out on me." Mindy looked both surprised and scared.

Karin stepped closer to Mindy, and she was furious. She tried to stem the flow of words but couldn't. "Mindy, what I'm saying has nothing to do with being mad at the world. I'm talking to you about one thing. I can shoot without help from you. Stop being a meddling little busybody."

Thick and eloquent silence pointed an accusing finger at Karin. Then a sob cut the silence, and another, as Mindy's nerves answered Karin's.

Without another word Karin turned and walked off the basketball court. She went down the hall into the shower room. She slumped down on a bench.

Why did I do that? she asked herself. Mindy's my best friend and I love her.

She heard the door open. She looked up at Miss Fletcher.

141

"What's the trouble, Karin?" Karin did not answer. "That wasn't at all like you, to talk like that to Mindy." Miss Fletcher sat down next to her. "I wish you'd talk things out with me. What's bothering you, Karin?"

"I don't know," she said slowly. Despite her answer, she did know why she didn't want to talk her troubles out with Miss Fletcher of all people. Truthfully, she was a little afraid of the coach, who had once been a good friend. Miss Fletcher was no longer a friend, she was Steve's sister. Furthermore, she was a mystery. Karin had no way of knowing how much she knew of what had happened between Steve and Karin, or what she thought about it, or how much she blamed Karin. Not to know was much worse than to know, for this way she mistrusted the coach. Since the night of the party, the relationship with Miss Fletcher had been embarrassing to Karin. It was hard to go out there on the basketball court and play under the supervision of a coach who was related to the boy who had rejected her.

That led her thoughts to something more subtle than her feelings toward Miss Fletcher. This conversation was floodlighting her feelings about Steve, stirring up latent thoughts, bringing them out into the open.

What's bothering me? she thought as she clamped her lips in a thin line. You want to know what's bothering me, Miss Fletcher? Well, it's that brother of yours. All right, so I was partly to blame, maybe, but I didn't do anything cruel. What Steve did to me was cruel and mean. And even if I forgave, I could never forget. I'll always remember the way he grabbed that knife and slashed my portrait. That's what's bothering me, Miss Fletcher, but I'll never let you know. Never!

So Miss Fletcher's next sentence surprised her. "Karin, I've deliberately kept out of the difficulty between you

142

and Steve. It hasn't been easy, because I love Steve and you must know I'm very fond of you."

Karin looked away. Miss Fletcher went on. "All this week I've watched your game going to pieces. Basketball is my business, Skeets. Your shots are bad, very bad. What have you got to say about it? I'm sure you want to clear things up and improve your game." Still no answer.

"Karin, let's get down to brass tacks and talk this thing through. If you don't care about basketball, I'm sure you care about Mindy. She's your best friend. What's bothering you so much that you'd turn on Mindy that way?"

"I don't know."

"Don't you want to talk to me about Steve?"

"I don't know."

"Don't you think you'd feel better if you got the whole thing off your chest?"

"I don't know."

"Karin, this isn't like you, sitting there and saying I don't know to everything. I want to talk to you and I want to help if I can."

For a second Karin almost relented. Miss Fletcher's persistence almost hacked through her crust of silence. Words, full of hurt and confusion and heartache, pounded for an outlet, but Karin stuffed them back. I won't talk, she thought. I'm not going to talk.

Miss Fletcher read her thoughts. "All right, if that's the way you want it. I want to help, but you're not giving me a chance." She got up from the bench and stood looking down at Karin.

"You're a very dangerous girl at this moment. To yourself and to others. If you won't let me help you personally, I can't force my help on you. But I'm still coach of this team, and I must protect the interests. A player is valuable only for what she contributes. Right now you're not con-

143

tributing anything. In fact, you're jeopardizing the team. You've thrown Mindy for a loop. Next it may be Carla, Babs, anyone."

She paused, then went on. "For the last time, will you talk this whole thing out with me, Karin? I'm waiting for an answer."

Karin looked up. "I don't think it would do any good. I'll apologize to Mindy after the practice," she said. "I'm sorry about that. But I don't want to talk about anything."

She saw the pulse beat in Miss Fletcher's jaw. "Very well, then," and the coach's voice was flat, decisive, "I have no alternative but to keep you on the bench during the Hanford game."

It was as if Miss Fletcher were a judge passing sentence. Karin heard the words, felt their finality, understood their significance. She was being disciplined until she could straighten herself out. She did not care. She suddenly did not care about anything.

She continued not to care. All during the ride over to Hanford while the other girls were feverish with excitement, keyed up to the boiling point over the big game ahead, Karin sat by herself, not talking, not joining in the chatter or the cheers or the school songs.

During the game she slumped on the bench where Miss Fletcher had sentenced her to sit, still not caring, her hands hanging limply in front of her, her eyes flashing from the court to the scoreboard and back again. It did not even matter that the game was close, fast, packed with suspense and surprises. In complete indifference, Karin watched the Rockridge team, which Greene Country was sure hadn't a chance in the world, defeat the favorite Hanford team by the narrow margin of 68–65 and thus become eligible for the state basketball finals.

144

KARIN HAD not lost much of her apathy when she took her seat on the bench for Rockridge's first game in the state tournament. She thought, It reminds me of Madison Square Garden and the circus.

This was the field house of the state university. It was the size of four gymnasiums, seating twelve thousand. Karin, looking around from her place on the Rockridge substitute bench, thought, I feel like the proverbial needle in the haystack. I don't think there's a spare seat and these are only the afternoon play-offs.

From where she sat, she could see and hear some of the confusion in the hallways. Out there, concession stands sold food and soft drinks, popcorn and cotton candy and hot dogs, banners, buttons, balloons.

Circus is right, she thought.

Karin's eyes found the section, not too far away, sporting the large Rockridge banner. Dozens of smaller Rockridge banners were waving above the heads of the crowd. Most of the town were here. Sixty miles was not too great a distance for them to go. So Karin's friends and neighbors had come in private cars and chartered buses. They had taken over most of the Savoy Hotel around the corner from the dormitory in which the Rockridge team was housed.

Karin's grandparents were here, and Oscar and the Ringquists. This morning, as they had got ready to leave, she had wryly commented, " I guess the only ones left in town will be Mamie and the fire department."

The trip had not been too pleasant. Karin had been glad to ride in the front seat between Oscar, driving, and Eric, who held her hand most of the way. In the back seat, solid as the sphinx and as silent had sat her grandparents. There had been a few sentences, now and then, about the weather, the roads, hotel accommodations. On the whole, however, this had not been the triumphal ride of a group of people headed for the final exciting games of a basketball tournament. It had been solemn and depressing, and Karin knew what the trouble was.

Her grandfather was disappointed in her. He tried not to show it. It was no use. He could no more hide his feelings than Karin could ever hide hers.

Her grandfather's disappointment in her bothered her. It was a kind of nagging worry inside her at this moment as she watched the officials go through the preliminary ritual of the tournament games. He wanted her to be in this game and here she sat on the bench.

Well, I've had my disappointments too, she thought. If he's going to love me only because I was making a big splash in basketball, that's not good enough. If all that closeness we built up can be smashed because I'm benched, then it couldn't have been worth very much.

Aside from these thoughts, she was feeling pretty good today. Her " benching " had given her a rest, a chance to slow down from the pressure, partly psychological, of being star forward of a team. The quarrel with Steve, although never completely out of her thoughts, had somewhat simmered down in her mind. She was still bothered but not so much. She was discovering that even heartbreak must have its turning point. Besides, Steve was not here at the tournament, of course. It was not the same as being afraid you might stumble over him at every turn in the school corridors.

So she was less tense today, much more relaxed than she had been during the games that followed the break with Steve. The hard core of indifference within her had spread, so she could detach herself from this circus, stand off, and see it with more perspective than one of those teammates of hers out there on the court.

The place was full of motion and light and color and noise — a kaleidoscope that swung each moment into a new pattern as the stands belched forth their cheers and shouts.

These were the quarter-finals, to be played this afternoon and evening. Eight teams would play off for the privilege of going, if they survived, into the semifinals tomorrow.

Of these eight teams, Rockridge rated lowest. No one expected them to survive this afternoon's game against one of the top teams in the state, Crestwood.

Karin watched the two teams line up. Crestwood appeared very self-assured. Her own teammates were serious and earnest. Karin saw Miss Fletcher standing in the side lines, talking with officials. She looked as sober as her team. The buzzer sounded. Karin stood with the crowd, faced the American flag and listened to the playing of the national anthem. The crowd sat down again as the referee hefted the ball for the center throw.

Karin heard the whistle above the din in the field house, saw the ball go into play. The pace of the game was astonishing. It was hard to follow the ball. Karin saw, however, that Rockridge had a worse case of tournament jitters than Crestwood. They could not seem to hang on to that ball.

The score built up fast — for Crestwood. At the end of the first quarter it stood 22–10. Of the Rockridge forwards, Babs was scoring heaviest, having thumped in three shots. Carla had made only one basket, and the other two points had been gained at the foul line.

They were doing as well as anyone had expected they would against this high-powered team from upstate.

147

In the second quarter, Rockridge surprised everyone by picking up. They started with a quick flurry of shots that almost evened the score in a very short time. Crestwood 25, Rockridge 20. The stands roared. It pleased the crowd to see the underdog move up.

Karin sat there, intent on the game. Babs was doing most of the heavy scoring. This figured. Babs was the least likely to be bowled over by this vast crowd. This was Babs's meat.

But how long will she last? Karin asked herself.

Her question was answered as the whistle blew. Karin heard the referee call: "Personal foul. Fairchild."

The foul shot was good. Crestwood 26, Rockridge 20.

Mindy made a basket with her scoop shot, 26–22.

Crestwood got the ball and lost it to Liz Ekstrom. Carla took it at the mid-line and heaved it in with a shoulder shot.

Crestwood 26, Rockridge 24.

The stands bellowed out a blast of encouragement.

"Move up and tie it, Rockridge!"

Karin leaned forward. All her indifference was gone. She watched the game go into the agonizing stage where each team is playing to the hilt, each scoring. First Crestwood would make a basket, then Rockridge. Rockridge never trailed by more than two points, sometimes by only one. It was almost too much to bear. Karin chewed her fingers at the nerve-racking closeness of the score.

She was rooting for her team now, rooting with everything in her. If Babs only holds out! she thought.

The whistle blew. "Personal foul. Fairchild. Charging."

Crestwood's free throws were good, but Carla canceled it out with another shoulder shot from 'way out on the floor.

"That's it," Karin muttered the words under her breath. "You're doing it, Carla. By the skin of your teeth, but you're doing it."

148

Carla dribbled in to shoot. Her momentum carried her off the court. Karin saw the danger at the same moment as Carla. On the side lines, directly in Carla's path, stood a small boy, a curious kid who had come out to get a better look. Every game had one. Carla lunged to the right of the boy, trying to avoid a body blow that would hurl him flat on his back. Carla's body twisted with violence and force. She missed the boy, but she went hurtling into space off balance, and landed on her left hip.

It was not a spectacular fall, but it was a heavy one. Carla got up. She limped back on the court. The whistle slashed into the game.

Karin was on her feet. She had to keep a tight grip on herself to stay off the court. She watched the doctors and Miss Fletcher hurry across the court to Carla. There was a quick examination. Carla limped off the floor to the deafening cheers of the spectators. Ellie Thompson went in for her.

The ball went back into play but for only a matter of seconds. Crestwood made one basket. The whistle blew for the intermission. At the end of the first half the score was Crestwood 35, Rockridge 32.

Karin was caught up in the confusion of the intermission. It took time to get to their headquarters. It took time for Miss Fletcher to talk to the doctors and learn that Carla's injury was a slight one, but she should stay out of the rest of this game. She could go back into the tournament tomorrow — if Rockridge survived.

Strange, Karin thought, as she heard those words, how quickly things change. A half hour ago anyone would have scoffed at the idea that Rockridge might play another game in this arena.

It took more time for Miss Fletcher to concentrate on Babs, pounding through her skull that she must, she absolutely must, watch her fouling. For once Babs seemed willing to listen.

"I'll put Ellie in for Carla again," Miss Fletcher said. "We'll spell the regular forwards from the substitute string. Jean Stivers will go in for Babs if she fouls again and we'll save Babs for the final spurt."

No one mentioned Karin. No one even looked her way.

She took her place on the bench as the second half began. It was murder — for Rockridge. With Carla out, the team was crippled. Ellie was no girl for this kind of game. Crestwood got the ball and kept getting it. They ran up eight points in the first couple of minutes. Karin watched the scoreboard.

Crestwood 43, Rockridge 32.

Mindy seemed nervous, off her game. Babs was watching it carefully, almost too carefully. Ellie didn't help much.

Karin was half out of her seat. She heard herself shout: "Mindy, get with those rebounds! Babs, take it at the midline! Hey, Ellie, you're playing basketball, not golf." Her voice was lost in the roars from the stands.

She slumped down on the bench, her throat dry and aching. Her hands itched, itched to get a grip on that piece of sweaty leather. Her eyes strained from the scoreboard to metal rim. A bursting agony of action swelled inside her, as it had in those early games when she spurred her team on to success. Only today she was tied to the bench.

For what? she asked herself. On account of a boy with paint up to his elbows!

She heard a sound at her right and glanced over toward the vacant half of the bench on which she sat. Miss Fletcher was sliding along it toward her. Karin stared, wondering.

The coach was next to her now, talking fast. "How do

you like what's going on out there?" she asked.

"I don't. The game's going down the drain."

"It needs your shooting eye, Karin. You haven't given us your best in a long time. Do you think you can forget your own personal problems long enough to get in there and shoot?"

A pause. Then, "Yes. I not only think, I *know*." Her hands itched, her nerves were raw with the frustration of delay.

"All right," Miss Fletcher's voice whipped out the words. "Go in for Ellie Thompson."

Karin reported to the officials' table and ran across the floor toward the referee. "Berglund for Thompson," she said. Ellie looked relieved.

Karin stood under the blaze of lights. She fastened her gaze on a dark spot in the polished wood floor. Today she did not look at the stands, those mountainous slopes of milling humanity. She felt like a tiny, helpless bug that had tumbled over a precipice and lay at the bottom of a gully.

But that feeling of total insignificance lasted only a second. The ball went into play, and she had only one thing on her mind during that last half of the game. To get it and *shoot*. She did not dare to think of a single other thing. Just get it and *shoot*, she kept telling herself. Just get your hands on that ball and *shoot!*

She had the fever again, that same driving urge to win that had gripped her in the Red Creek game. This time, however, she did not feel that contagious spark go out to her teammates. If she was aware of one other thing besides that ball, it was Mindy and Babs, watching her. And Liz and Deedie and Jean. They looked worried to see her on the floor, not elated, not even pleased, just plain worried.

151

They're waiting for me to prove myself, she thought. All right, I will.

She got the ball. It came to her from Mindy, above the head of her guard. Karin jumped and caught it. She held it between her fingers, the old way, the good way. She pivoted, feinted, dribbled. Now, now take aim and let go.

She did. It was a clean shot, right through the rim. The net swished. She walked back to get ready for the next play. The noise in the field house was deafening, but she did not mind it any more. She hardly heard it. It was like background music, something that was there, yet wasn't there. But it did not reach her.

She watched the ball. That's all that mattered now, watching that ball and getting it. She racked up the score. She was at top form, playing better basketball than she had in weeks. She knew she was doing well. Everything fell into place, all at once. Everything jelled. She was *with* it!

She didn't watch the scoreboard, didn't worry about time. She kept her mind on the one thing Miss Fletcher had sent her in here to do. She used her shooting eye to drop the ball through the rim.

She saw Mindy make a few baskets. She breathed a silent hope that Babs would last out the game. But above everything else, above points and time and shots and scoreboards was the driving urge to do one thing, to play a perfect game of basketball.

For the game itself, for nothing but the game.

She almost did not hear the final buzzer when it came. Her first awareness that the game was over came from Mindy who threw her arms around Karin and, half hysterical, shouted at her, " Skeets, we won, we won! "

Karin shook her head, coming out of the daze. She felt suddenly dog-tired, every muscle ached, every nerve

152

throbbed. Yet above this exhaustion was a glow of satisfaction, not only because Babs and Mindy and the others were gathering around, shouting their fool heads off, but because of something inside her that said well done!

She looked into the flushed and sweaty faces around her. " What was the score? " she asked.

" Look! Look, Skeets, see for yourself." Mindy swung her around toward the giant scoreboard. There, in blazing letters she read it. " Crestwood 59, Rockridge 62."

CHAPTER | 16

THIS WAS the night of the semifinals.

The Rockridge team had an early supper together at one end of the dining room in their dormitory. Some of the girls ate heartily; others hardly touched their food.

Karin noticed that Carla was in the latter group. This afternoon she had been examined again by the tournament doctors and they had unanimously decided that Carla could carry on tonight. Yet, Karin thought, she did not appear to be her usual buoyant self.

In fact, Karin found it interesting to note the effect of increasing pressure on all the girls. She felt it herself. Yesterday they had been the one team that was sure to be eliminated in the quarter-finals. Tonight they were the dark horse that was galloping into the limelight.

On the streets this afternoon, as they had gone sightseeing together, total strangers had pointed them out. " Those are the Rockridge girls. They beat Crestwood, one of the top teams in the state. Think they'll last through the semifinals? "

No one was happier about this sudden turn of events than Karin's grandfather. He had found her after the game yesterday, had thrown his arms around her, and had shouted: "Karin, my girl, you were wonderful! Yah, just wonderful."

She had eased out of his hearty embrace as gracefully and as fast as she could — so many people were watching — and she had thought, almost rebelliously: Thanks, Gramp, for liking me when I'm winning. I wish you'd love me half as much when I'm in the doghouse.

Tonight the Rockridge team went to the field house early. They huddled together on the benches and watched Madison play Westover. Westover won, as all the experts had predicted they would.

Karin's eyes almost popped when she saw the Westover girls in action. This was the far-famed number-one team of the state and she could understand the reason for its reputation.

The girls played the kind of basketball Rockridge had played in one or two games, when they were at their peak, only better. Their ball-handling was smooth. Their floor work was graceful and efficient. Their set plays were precisely done, not a hitch anywhere. They had the fastest moving offense Karin had ever seen in a girls' game. They had good jumping guards who were almost perfect at rebounds, thus making tip-ins all but impossible. In short, they had everything.

When they ran off the court, having defeated Madison, 72–60, the booming plaudits of the crowd of twelve thousand followed them.

Karin took her place with her team for the warmup. Despite the tension, which they all felt, inevitably, she was even more at ease on the basketball court tonight than she had been yesterday afternoon. She was used now to

154

this cavernous place, full of strange sights and sounds. The brief shock of " tournament jitters " that had gripped her in the first few seconds yesterday did not bother her to-night.

She ran along the line of forwards, taking the ball, shoot-ing, catching, throwing it to the next in line. Her control was excellent. She made all but one of the baskets she tried.

The game began. Tonight Rockridge was playing Clin-ton, a team from the southeast corner of the state. Clinton was, without a doubt, one of the top teams in the tourna-ment. Until a week ago it had been in some ways even stronger than Westover. Then it had run into a streak of crippling handicaps. First, its strongest guard had been in-volved in an automobile accident. Then, two of its best reserve guards had come down with intestinal flu. Last night Karin and her teammates had watched Clinton play in the quarter-finals. Throughout the game, Stretch Simp-son, the number-one scorer on the team, seemed bothered by something. She had shown signs of fatigue and of diffi-culty in getting into her stride. Her shots had been good, ofttimes spectacular, but it was clear that she was strain-ing.

Then word had come this morning that Stretch Simpson had come down with the intestinal flu that was plaguing this team. Clinton had reserves, but whether these would be strong enough to carry them through to victory this evening was an open question. It made the Rockridge-Clin-ton game one of the most exciting in this tournament.

From the starting whistle, it was clear that in this game, Rockridge had the edge on Clinton. Although Clinton took the center throw at the start and hurled it deep into their territory toward their basket-hanging forwards, Liz Eks-trom intercepted and sent the ball back to Carla at the mid-line. It went back and forth from Carla to Mindy to Carla and then to Karin near the basket, but the guards, forming a tight knot near the shooting area, blocked her shot and she had to get rid of it. The ball passed from one of the Rockridge forwards to another and then Karin, moving out on the floor, got it.

I'll have to use a hook shot! It's the only thing these leeches can't stop, she thought. She let go a hook shot. This was her night because it landed straight through the basket, clean, for a score.

The game became a tight one. First Rockridge would score, then Clinton. The spectators were on their feet, excited, thundering their encouragement. It was the kind of game the stands loved, tight, close, hard fought.

Carla called time out. Miss Fletcher met her team at the side-line huddle. "We can leave Clinton 'way behind if we use our heads," she said. "Number one, their defense is weakening. Two, they're using tight zone defense around the basket in order to save their strength. This gives us an advantage. We can throw those guards in a tizzy by bringing them out to the corners, then back to the basket, then out again, then back. They haven't the strength or the reserves for man-to-man defense. So this is it. Karin will take the ball out into the corners. Karin can manage floor shots from any angle. She's in top form tonight." A nod and smile showed the sincerity of the compliment.

"Now the rest of you, Mindy, Carla, Babs, Ellie, whoever is in, will deliberately drive toward Karin in the corner, feed her the ball. Let her shoot from there until you have the guards all out to get Karin, then drive back toward the basket. Mindy, get the rebounds. Carla and Karin try a variety of shots, and, Karin, you take the tip-ins. When you've got Clinton glued to the basket area, drive out again to Karin in the corners. Do you get it?"

156

"Yes," Carla answered for the team, "it'll drive the Clinton guards stark-raving mad."

Miss Fletcher nodded, pleased. "That's what we're hoping for."

The whistle called them back to the game. The Clinton team looked tired and worried. The ball came over to the Rockridge forwards.

They played it Miss Fletcher's way, a hard, controlled, brainy game. When they got the ball, which was often, Karin took it deep into the corners for a high, looping corner shot from a point parallel to the backboard. These were rim shots, real swishers through the net.

The Clinton guards were kept distracted as Rockridge changed its tactics from long shots to driving lay-up shots. They were not equal to the swift change of pace.

At the quarter the board read 19–15 and at the half 32–22, both times in favor of Rockridge.

The intermission crowd milled out into the corridors. Karin, caught up in it, was separated from her team. She was pushing her way through the crowd outside Clinton's headquarters when she heard her name.

"Karin, Karin!" She turned to find her grandfather and the Ringquists, Oscar, and some people she did not recognize.

Her grandfather put his arm around her shoulder. His speech was rich with his Swedish cadence, as always when he was stirred. "Karin, I am so proud of you." He turned to the people nearby whom Karin had never met.

"This is my granddaughter. From the East, she came out to live with us." He rolled off the names of his friends. "She's a real Berglund, yah?"

Karin wanted to get away, to stop the flow of words. This kind of thing always embarrassed her, especially in public, and she could see from the corner of her eye a

157

group of boys, troublemakers no doubt, huddling around the door of the Clinton headquarters. Friends of the Clinton girls, they would be looking for any excuse to poke fun at a Rockridge girl. She knew these boys recognized her for she heard one of them say: " That's Berglund. The star forward who's doing all the fancy work tonight."

She wanted to end this conversation as fast as she could. " Gramp, I've got to go, honestly. It's been nice to meet you," she said to his friends. But he would not let her off so easily. He kept hold of her, detaining her, unwilling to take his arm from her shoulder.

" Gramp, honestly, I'll be late."

" There is time," he insisted. " I want everyone to see you. I'm proud of you, Karin. I want to show you off."

There was a snicker from the group of Clinton boys. She got away at last, but as she hurried past them, they whistled after her and called: " Good-by, Grandpa's girl. Hey, Grandpa's girl, what's your hurry? "

It was a mean thing to have happen, and it jarred her. The intermission, which should have been a time of rest and charging up, was wasted on her. She sat in the huddle with her teammates, listening to Miss Fletcher's instructions but hearing the taunts of the Clinton boys ringing in her ears.

" Skeets." She glanced up. " It's the buzzer for us to get back to the court." Mindy was waiting for her. The others had already filed out of the team room. " What's wrong, Skeets? You look as if you'd seen a ghost."

" Maybe I have," she muttered as they started back to the big gym. " Maybe I have."

They were crossing the floor to take their places on the court when Mindy grabbed Karin's arm. " If you think you've seen one ghost, take a good look over there by Miss Fletcher and you'll be sure you've seen another."

158

Karin looked where Mindy pointed. It was Steve! No, she thought. It can't be Steve. Not here, not at the basketball tournament.

But it was Steve all right. He was standing with his sister, talking to her, and she was beaming.

Now I have two things to bother me, Karin thought. The ghost of Ed Berglund's granddaughter and Steve Fletcher.

"I wonder what ever made him change his mind and come," Mindy said, staring goggle-eyed at Steve.

"Come on," Karin pulled Mindy away, steering her across the court. "The second half's going to begin."

The whistle blew. Clinton took the center throw. This time they kept the ball, sending it deep into their own side of the court. Within split seconds, they had passed it from forward to forward and tossed it through the basket for two points. Liz, overeager, made bodily contact on the shot. Clinton was given one free throw. Their foul shot was good.

Rockridge 32, Clinton 25.

In less than one minute, Clinton had scored three points. Karin took the ball for Rockridge. She fumbled and almost lost it, recovered, had to get rid of it because of her guard and sent it to Carla. It went to Mindy, back to Carla while Karin moved into the corner, parallel to the backboard for a long shot. She jumped for the ball, caught it over the head of her guard. As she raised the ball for her long corner shot, she saw instantly that something was wrong with her control. It wasn't as steady as it had been during the first half when she had whammed them in one after another.

She watched the high loop of the ball as it sailed toward the basket. It teetered for one breath-taking moment. She could feel the crowd take in its breath. The ball dropped off into the hands of a Clinton guard. She ran, trying to intercept the ball as it passed from guard to guard. Clinton kept the ball. It went back over the mid-line to Clinton's forwards. A tall girl near the basket got it and tapped it easily in.

Rockridge 32, Clinton 27.

She had given Clinton those two points on a silver platter.

The ball came to her again, this time she got it deep in the opposite corner, shaking her guard. Again she raised it for a long shot, again her co-ordination was off. The ball did not even hit the rim.

Carla and a Clinton guard jumped for it. The guard swatted it toward the waiting hands of another Clinton guard and again there was that plunge for it as it went over the mid-line toward the Clinton forwards. Liz and Deedie and Sue struggled for possession, but Clinton kept it. A long shot sent it into the basket from 'way out on the court.

Rockridge 32, Clinton 29.

She had handed Clinton another two points on the same silver platter. Her own teammates were still feeding her the ball, as Miss Fletcher had directed. This time she caught it on the jump, and it slipped through her fingers. She recovered the ball, but a piercing voice shot through the field-house grandstands.

" Grandpa's girl! Hey, Grandpa's girl, you put grease on your hands during intermission? "

There was a wave of laughter. And the dreadful epithet echoed and re-echoed. Grandpa's girl. Grandpa's girl.

Karin raised the ball for her long corner shot. Her hands trembled. She tried to control them and couldn't. She missed the basket by a good two feet. Mindy caught the ball. Carla called time out.

Karin thought Miss Fletcher would take her out of the

160

game. She didn't. She sent Babs in for Mindy who was showing signs of fatigue, but she left Karin in.

"Stay close to the basket and tap them in," she told Karin. "Carla will take the corner shots. You handle those near the basket. Babs, you stay with Karin." As they came out of the huddle, Miss Fletcher whispered to her: "Roll with the punches, Karin. Take that stuff in your stride. Don't let it throw you."

She tried. She honestly tried, but her high-powered game was gone. She knew for sure the next time she got the ball. The steady eye for which she was famous, the absolute control over that slippery hunk of leather, was shattered. Her hands shook. She could not heave the ball in. Behind those trembling hands was her inner turmoil. Two things bothered her, and she could not let them roll off: The ghost of Ed Berglund's granddaughter, risen from the mocking "Grandpa's girl" that had been shouted from the stands, and the fact that Steve Fletcher sat out there close to the side lines, watching her, hearing those catcalls from the stands as her game went to pieces.

She strained and tightened up. She missed her shots right and left.

The scoreboard told the story at the end of the third quarter. Rockridge 38, Clinton 40.

Miss Fletcher did not waste words scolding Karin, and once again to Karin's surprise, she did not take her out.

"Carla, we'll take a long chance," the coach said. "Sometimes a team has to do just that. If it works, we'll win."

"What's that, Miss Fletcher?" Carla asked.

"We'll use screening. Carla will be our attack. One of the other forwards will get between her and her guard, practically guarding Carla. If the Clinton guard tries to come between Carla and the forward who's guarding her,

161

the Clinton guard will surely foul. She'll have to hit one of you."

"It would have to be a girl who knew how to guard," Carla said doubtfully.

"Right." Miss Fletcher swung on Karin. "You guarded back East, Karin. Do you think you can screen for Carla?"

"Yes," she replied, "I'm sure I can." Anything, she thought, anything to take the strain of shooting off me.

"Carla," Miss Fletcher went on, "use your shoulder shot, from way out. Babs, stay near the basket for rebounds." She gave them each a clap on the shoulder for moral support as they went back to the game.

It worked. Whenever Rockridge got the ball, Carla, with Karin screening her, sent it zooming for the basket. Two things saved them. The lead they had made during the first half when Karin was really with it, and Clinton's weakened defense. When the final buzzer sounded, the scoreboard read Rockridge 54, Clinton 50.

They were still in the tournament. It had been no smashing victory. It had cost them a lot. Carla and Babs were exhausted. Despite their victory, Karin felt the taste of personal defeat in her mouth. Even when her teammates patted her on the back and said: "You did a good job, Skeets, screening that way for Carla. You're the only one who could have done that," it did not dispel the bitterness. She herself was the best judge of what had happened to her. She had seen her trembling hands. She had blown up on her game.

What made it even harder to take was the fact that Steve had sat there through the entire debacle.

On the way down to the showers, Carla, breathing hard, limped beside Karin. "Your leg hurt?" Karin asked.

"A little. Funny, it was fine till that last quarter. Skeets, we're still in this tournament, but I feel more scared than glad. I don't think I could get through another game like that."

Karin answered with great deliberation. "You don't think you *can* get through one. Me, I don't think I *want* to!"

CHAPTER | 17

TOURNAMENT COACHES made it a practice to keep their teams isolated from families and friends. Miss Fletcher observed this rule with slight modifications. Telephone calls were permitted. If they wished, the girls might spend a couple of hours in the afternoon with their families. Boy friends, however, were out of bounds.

On the afternoon of the tournament finals, Karin called her grandfather at his hotel and asked to be excused from going over.

"I didn't sleep too well, Gramp," she told him. "I need some rest before the game tonight."

"You could come a little while, Karin."

"Gramp, I don't think I'd better. You've got people all over the place and it means excitement. I'd never calm down."

"All right, Karin. We'll see you at the game, then."

She came out of the phone booth in the dormitory, deeply disturbed. Something in her grandfather's voice troubled her, a flat disappointment and wistful longing.

I couldn't have done it, she thought. Not if I'm going to stay in that game tonight. Gramp stirs me up, with his Grandpa's girl stuff, showing me off to everyone.

If I'd gone over there, something would have happened to throw me off my game again. I can't afford that risk.

163

Last night was a close call and we were only playing Clinton. Tonight it's Westover. Westover, the perfect girls basketball team.

She started down the hall of the dormitory, knowing that the room she shared with her teammates would be empty at this time of day and she could get some much-needed rest. As she was crossing the reception room, she saw a boy standing there. Preoccupied, she looked away, then she thought, That's funny, a boy in this place. Boys are strictly taboo.

She glanced back sharply and saw who it was. She was so surprised that his name tumbled out. " Steve! "

" Hello," he came toward her. " I was waiting for you. They told me you'd come back this way. Karin, I want to talk to you. Please."

" She did not look at him as she answered. " Boys are out of bounds. I guess you know that."

" I got permission from the coach." She turned toward him and saw his faint smile. " I convinced her it was important enough to break a rule, and besides she's my sister, you know."

" I know." She moved away, toward the far end of the room. It was unlikely any of the girls would saunter through this time of day, but if they did, she wanted to be sure she and Steve would be out of earshot. Steve followed her.

" I bet you're wondering why I'm here at the tournament." She nodded. " Well I heard you won the quarter-finals, and I wanted to be here for the rest. To give my moral support to my sister and — well, maybe you won't believe this — but to you especially, Karin."

She stared at him, unbelieving. " It took you an awfully long time to make up your mind."

" I came to help, Karin. Honestly."

164

"It doesn't help, Steve." She moved away. "It's too late. It doesn't help at all."

"If I told you that I'm sorry, very, very sorry about what I did that night, Karin, would you believe me?"

"Yes, but it wouldn't make any difference. It's as I said, Steve, it's too late."

He moved closer. "It's never too late, Karin. People make mistakes. Big mistakes, sometimes. That's only human. In life you've got to do what you do in a math class, erase the mistake from the board and try again."

"But what about the Berglunds who swashbuckle their way through Greene County as if they owned the air everybody breathed? The Berglunds who sit in their big house and expect people to run and dance when they whistle? And what about the boy who doesn't want my love because it's too selfish and possessive, Steve?"

"I've been trying to tell you that I've changed. I've had time to think things through since that night. I'm not the same person I was then. I'm trying to tell you that I care about you, Karin. A whole lot."

"And I'm telling you that I've changed too, Steve. I'm telling you that I don't care."

She turned, ran past him up the stairs to her room. She flung open the door, hurled herself into the big bedroom with its rows of cots and flung herself face down on the nearest one. There, in the silence of the empty room, she released the great, tearless sobs that racked her body but left her eyes dry.

She sobbed herself to sleep. She was awakened by her name called from a distance. "Karin Berglund. Karin Berglund." She opened her eyes and saw someone standing at the foot of the cot. It was one of the housemothers. She looked anxious. "Are you all right?" she asked.

"Yes. I must have been awfully tired and fell asleep."

165

"There's someone to see you."

Karin jumped up, straightening her skirt, pulling down her sweater. Not Steve again I hope, she thought. Then a more disturbing thought gripped her. It might be her grandfather.

"He said to tell you that it's Oscar."

Ozzie, good old Ozzie!

"I've asked him to wait in the small private reception room reserved for conferences," the housemother said. "I thought you might be able to talk better there."

"Thank you." Karin found a comb and ran it through her hair. "I'll go right down."

When she saw Oscar, his open smile welcoming her, she broke down. He opened his arms and she ran to him, and this time the sobs brought tears. She seemed a child again, finding comfort in her father's arms.

"There, there, you be a woman for a few minutes and cry your heart out," he said. "Then we talk a little, Karin."

She broke away, sniffling. "I'm all right," she said, fishing in her pocket for tissues. "I feel better now that you're here. How did you guess that I needed you, Ozzie?"

"We sit down and talk." She sat with him on one of the sofas. "Now, what is this? You tell me what the matter is. You will not come to see your grandfather. And Steve, he comes tearing into my room, like a crazy fellow, raving about you. He wants to patch up the quarrel and you run away from him." When she didn't reply, he said, "You love him very much, yah?"

"I don't believe in love any more. Steve taught me not to."

"So we talk a little about love, then." He reached for her hand, holding it. "Love is more than this, Karin, more than having someone hold your hand, or having a person that you are fond of with you. It has got to be inside first.

It is not so much the way someone feels about you, but the way you feel about others."

"I feel hurt and misunderstood, Ozzie. And let down."

"Let down, you say? Then, that is because you are looking at what is wrong in the other people. You have got to change that and look at others for what is best in them. You have got to see what is right about the people you love and not what is wrong about them."

"I don't know what you mean."

"Take your grandfather, for instance. You see him a proud man, too proud maybe, and domineering. He bosses. He wants his own way. So he cannot help that; it is just the way he is. But he has lots of good things about him too."

"I know he has, but these bad things get in the way."

"You must not let them. And take Steve. Steve has a temper and he is selfish and he changes. As many phases as the moon that boy has. Too smart for his own good, with a quick tongue and sometimes an answer that hurts. Well, he is artistic, so he has the temperament that goes with it. You going to hold this against him? You going to be so blinded by Steve's faults that you cannot see that he is a strong person and a real intelligent boy who can be something someday?" Oscar nodded his head in emphasis. "And Steve is big, Karin, he sees things big. It takes a big man to come to you and say he was wrong. You should be big too and forgive."

"I forgave him long ago. But I can't forget. Never. All my life I'll remember that night and what Steve did."

"Then you have not forgiven. So long as you can remember a wrong, Karin, you have not honestly forgiven. You have to forget before you can forgive."

She sat with him in silence a few moments, digesting what he had said. Then she patted his hand: "Thanks,

167

Ozzie. Thanks for being honest with me."

"I will go back now," he said, getting up. "You throw off all this bad feeling inside you, Karin, and tonight you play the best game of your life."

"I'd better!" she said. "We're playing the strongest team in the state. Everyone is sure they've got us licked already."

"Not me! I will sit up there in that grandstand shouting my head off and tossing my hat up in the air for you."

"Thanks," she had to laugh at him. "You're the most wonderful person in the world, Ozzie, except maybe my own father." She kissed him on the cheek. "I love you, you big *svensk*, you."

He smiled, tickled. "Yah, you laugh again. That is good. Tonight you will play *free*."

She left Oscar and went back along the corridors of the dormitory toward her room. She felt stirred, restless, as if Oscar had injected some chemical into her system that was transforming her entire nature.

At the door of the room someone stopped her. She was so deep in thought that it took a moment for the words she heard to sink in.

It was Mindy, grabbing her arm and saying: "Skeets, it's awful. Have you heard the news? Carla's sick. The game last night was too much of a strain, and the doctors have taken her out of the tournament."

168

THE FIELD HOUSE was once again packed to capacity for this final game of the tournament. Karin stood on the Rockridge side of the court and watched the toss of the coin. Rockridge won. They took the throw on the second and fourth quarters.

Her eyes made one final sweep of the stands back of where Miss Fletcher was stationed. No sign of Steve. Tonight she was as disturbed by his absence as she had been last night by his presence. She wanted to talk to him. She had tried to reach him by telephone at the Savoy Hotel, but he was not there.

Maybe he had gone home. That would be too bad. After Oscar's conversation with her, she felt she had unfinished business with Steve, things that had to be said now or she might never say them.

She shifted uneasily about the court, waiting for the whistle and the center throw. Westover looked good, too good. All the assurance was on that side of the court. Her teammates looked grim and tense. So much was against them. At best, they played an uneven game, sometimes brilliant, sometimes sloppy. Their varsity forwards were, at their peak, terrific shots, but they were a little tired from the excitement of the tournament, and Carla Peterson was out of this game. This might put an insurmountable strain on Babs and Mindy and Karin. Rockridge's reserves were not strong. They did not, like Westover, have three or four hard-hitting teams that could spell one another.

Karin let her glance wander again toward where Steve should have been. Still not there. " Get with it, Skeets. This

169

is it." It was Mindy telling her to keep her mind on the game.

The whistle blew. Westover's forward took the ball on the center throw, tossed it to a teammate, ran to receive it, then tossed it to the third Westover forward and it went straight to the basket. Plop. A clean shot. It had been done as neatly as if they were target-practicing.

Whew! Karin thought. What passing and floor work. If this is a sample, it's going to be murder.

The ball was in play again, this time Rockridge's possession. The Westover guards had a tight, aggressive defense but Babs, Mindy, and Karin kept the ball, passing it, maneuvering for the chance to shoot. Karin made a line violation. The whistle blew. The referee gave Westover the ball out of bounds. It whizzed back into Westover territory for a long, accurate shot into the basket. Westover 4, Rockridge 0.

Karin waited for the ball to go into play. There was thick silence on her side of the court. Babs and Mindy did not chide her for the sloppy footwork that had given Westover those two points. She almost wished they would.

Again the ball came to Rockridge. It passed from Babs to Mindy, back to Babs, then to Karin. She had to get rid of it because of her towering guard, so she sent it to Mindy. Mindy hurled it to Karin again, sending it to her at the spot where she could easily have caught it on the run. Karin's timing was off, 'way off, and the ball slipped from her fingers into the waiting hands of the Westover guard. It went back across Westover's mid-line. A tremendous court shot from their tallest forward sent it to a basket hanger who tapped it in. Westover 6, Rockridge 0.

As Karin went to her position on the court, Mindy called, "What's the matter tonight, Skeets? Come on, let's rack up a few for our side."

170

She winced at the rebuke but did not reply. Mindy was right. If she could keep her mind on the game instead of wondering about that empty space behind Miss Fletcher, she'd do better.

Babs called over, " Skeets, are you forgetting you're acting captain? "

That roused her. She had almost forgotten! With Carla out, it was her job to call fixed floor plays. She flashed signals to Babs and Mindy, indicating that they'd use Miss Fletcher's figure-eight pattern. Mindy and Babs signaled that they'd got it. The ball came to them and they kept it. Their endless routines of floor plays came to their rescue. With Karin awake, and the Rockridge guards in top form, Rockridge began to score. Mindy sank two. Babs tossed in a couple. At the end of the first quarter the scoreboard read: Westover 15, Rockridge 10.

Karin had made the other two points at the foul line. Her floor shots, however, had been something less than sensational.

As she crossed the court for the two-minute break, Liz Ekstrom got her ear. " Are you planning to shoot any during this game, captain? Or are you leaving the heavy scoring to Mindy and Babs? "

The second quarter went much as the first, with Westover held down by the fighting spirit of the Rockridge guards, with Rockridge scoring some but lagging behind. The half ended with a score of 26–22 in favor of Westover. Most of the Rockridge shots had been made by Mindy, Babs, and a couple by Ellie, who had gone in for a few minutes to relieve Babs.

Karin was still not on her game. As the clock ticked off the last minute of play for the first half, she saw Steve. She was waiting to receive the ball at the mid-line, but in her excitement, she fumbled and lost it.

171

The buzzer ended the half. She glanced again at the scoreboard. Westover was only four points ahead, not a tremendous lead, but it was enough. Enough to win them the game in the last half when they could dip into their strong reserves while Rockridge went down under shooting fatigue.

She looked at her teammates. The guards were holding up. Miss Fletcher had been able to send in reserves to relieve Sue and Deedie for a few minutes of play. Liz did not seem to need this relief. She was playing better than ever.

The forwards showed the greatest strain. They missed Carla, and Karin had not been much use except at the foul line. How long Babs and Mindy could bear the brunt of scoring, Karin did not know. She had spent this half feeding and screening, giving Babs and Mindy the ball as much as possible. She had not trusted herself to shoot.

It was a psychological block, a hang-over from yesterday's game when she had let grandstand heckling and personal problems throw her.

She was halfway across the court, on her way out of the gym for the intermission when she heard Liz's voice needling her.

"Skeets," and she gave the nickname a slurring tone, "maybe you'd rather be on our side of the court. Maybe you think you're still playing guard for that team you played on back East. You weren't good for much else than screening during that half we just played."

Karin wheeled on Liz, ready to let her have it. Her hands trembled, she felt the tingle of sharp anger flash through her body.

No, she told herself, it's not Liz. It's me. And I know what the trouble is.

You've got to look at others for what is right in them,

172

not for what is wrong. That was the gist of what Oscar had told her. She had been seeing what was wrong about Steve, about her grandfather, the people closest to her. This was her mistake. Oscar had said she must see the best in others, not the worst. And she must forgive. So long as she remembered a wrong, she had not forgiven.

It was a large order. She was not sure she could do it. She would never be sure she could do it until she went over there where Steve Fletcher was sitting and tried it out.

She broke from the line of teammates. "Hey," Mindy called, "where you going, Skeets?"

"I've got something to take care of," she said. That was the truth. She had something to take care of, some unfinished business before she could go into the last half of this game. She stopped Miss Fletcher on her way out. "May I have permission to be a minute late for the huddle between halves?" she asked, her eyes pleading as much as her voice. "It's important."

Miss Fletcher nodded and turned, watching Karin as she raced across the court to where Steve was sitting. They faced each other, each waiting.

"Hi," she said. "I tried to call you up, Steve." He was waiting for her, apparently having said all he had to say. She gulped, pulled in a deep breath and said the words fast, eagerly, before she lost her nerve.

"I was wrong too," she sputtered. "I never meant to be bossy or possessive or to know it all." She hesitated. "And I didn't mean what I said this afternoon about not caring." She paused. The words she had come here to say were pushing against her, trying to tumble out in their eagerness to be heard. Yet she took her time because this was what she had come here to say, and it must be right, exactly right, or it would do more harm than good. It was

173

a little like aiming for a hook shot from 'way out on the court. You had to be sure and accurate the first time. There was only one chance to shoot.

"Steve, I guess loving someone is about the hardest thing in the world to do right. Because we always sort of want the people we love to be perfect. And that's all wrong. Because if they were perfect, they'd be awful, and we'd never love them in the first place."

She turned and ran out of the gym, fast, fast as she could go, but she had the satisfaction of knowing that Steve's eyes had answered her, if his voice had not, and she had seen something in them she had never seen before. A thing called tenderness.

She was a different girl when the buzzer called them back to the floor for the second half.

It was Westover's ball on the center throw. It went into their half of the court, from forward to forward. Liz, jumping for it, intercepted, caught it. A mighty yell went up from the Rockridge team at this lucky break. The screams from the stands cheered Liz.

She sent it back over the mid-line and Karin was there to catch it. She wheeled, held it above her head, was tempted to pass to Babs, then decided to shoot. Karin held it that split second, aimed, with that deadly accurate aim she had at her best, and let go. It whirled through space, a high arc, looping toward the basket. It teetered, then dropped in. The stands let up a roar.

"Pretty," Mindy shouted to Karin. "That's the way, Skeets."

Again Westover got the ball. This time it was Deedie who took it away from them on a rebound. She turned, hesitated, saw Karin at the mid-line, sent a long, spectacular pass to her. Karin jumped to catch it. She turned, dribbled, looked for an opening to Babs or Mindy near

174

the basket. They were closely guarded.

I'll try it again, she thought. She hooked it this time, a strong, sure shot from the corner and again it plopped through the netting. Again the stands let out a roar.

"That's the stuff, Grandpa's girl," some wit shouted. She shook it off. It didn't reach her the way it had yesterday.

She glanced up at the scoreboard: 26–26. She had tied the score in the first minute of the third quarter.

Westover took the ball again, held it this time, and racked up two points, breaking the tie. Then Babs fouled and Westover scored another point.

The board read: Westover 29, Rockridge 26.

Karin got the ball. She sent it to Mindy, who tossed it to Babs, then it came back to Karin. She tried for another long shot, and again it was good.

Westover 29, Rockridge 28. The stands were screaming.

Westover took the ball, they sent it in long, driving passes toward the basket, a forward taking it near enough to tap it in. The forward slipped, lost her balance, and the ball rebounded. Deedie got it and tossed it to Liz, who sent it to Karin at the mid-line. She turned, pivoted, raised her arms for a throw and the guard, overeager to stop another long shot, touched Karin's arm.

The referee's whistle cut into the game. "Lawson, personal foul." The referee's arm sawed the air, to indicate hacking. "Two free throws. Berglund take it."

Karin stepped to the foul line. Her long shots from the court were good now, but could she have that same control at the foul line? With that mob screaming at her, booing, whistling, heckling. "Can you sink them, Grandpa's girl?"

She rubbed her sweaty hands on her shorts. Take your time, don't let them throw you. Easy does it, no need to hurry.

175

She held the ball between her fingers, took aim, let it go. Plop. The scoreboard clicked a point.

Westover 29, Rockridge 29.

Bedlam from the stands.

The ball came to her again. She held it in one hand, wiping the other, as much from nervousness as anything. Then she gripped the ball lightly, broadened her stance, and shot. It swished through. It was good.

Westover 29, Rockridge 30.

It was the first time Rockridge had gone ahead in this game. The stands were a madhouse.

The game took on the grim quality of suspense that tightened nerves both on the court and in the spectators' galleries. It seesawed back and forth. First Westover shot ahead, then Rockridge. Just before the buzzer ended the third quarter, Westover sank a foul shot that put them ahead one point.

The scoreboard read 43–42.

Karin had borne the brunt of that quarter and she felt it. She was panting as she went into the huddle during the two-minute break. There was little talking. Miss Fletcher did not launch into a series of instructions. There was no attempt at a long pep talk. All she said was: " Keep up the good work, girls. You're doing fine. Give it all you've got."

Smart coach, Karin thought. It's a wise one who knows when to keep still!

Rockridge had the advantage of the center throw on the fourth quarter. They got the ball and kept it. Mindy scooped it in for a clean shot. Westover 43, Rockridge 44.

Westover took the ball, sent it from forward to forward in that storm-the-citadel pass work of theirs. It went in. Westover 45, Rockridge 44.

The old seesaw is on again! Karin thought.

She took it at the foul line when a Westover guard

pushed her. Westover 45, Rockridge 45.

The playing was tight now, guards on both sides holding their own, preventing the forwards from piling up the shots. For several minutes neither side scored in the unbroken tie.

Then Babs, bulling her way in a great spurt, held the ball and sank one. Westover 45, Rockridge 47.

Westover got the ball and Sue, straining to intercept, was charged with pushing. The Westover forward took two shots at the foul line. One missed, but the other was good.

Westover 46, Rockridge 47.

The game jumped back and forth again. When Karin had the chance to look at the scoreboard it read Westover 55, Rockridge 56. She glanced at the clock. Two minutes to play. The ball was Rockridge's. This was a break. If they held it and fed it to her in the corner, she could probably sink it in easily the way she was playing this game, and that shot would clinch their lead by three points.

She glanced from the clock to her teammates to see how they were standing up. Babs was doing well, very well. She had watched her fouling throughout this game, played it cool, safe, and steady. Mindy was white with strain, and Miss Fletcher might under other circumstances have taken her out, but not this time, not so close to the finish.

That would have been dangerous psychologically, and the coach knew it.

Karin called to Mindy and Babs. " One more shot will do it for us. Feed it to me in the corner."

The ball came toward her and she jumped for it. Her guard was too quick. She got the ball and sent it over the mid-line toward her waiting forward. The forward pivoted, feinted as if to pass, then shot, an arching shoulder shot for the basket and it was good.

Westover 57, Rockridge 56.

The stands were on their feet, screaming, howling.

Karin felt herself go limp. That could be the shot that determined the game. The clock showed a minute and a half left. The ball was Rockridge's. It went to Mindy, to Babs, then to Karin in the corner where she had instructed them to feed it to her. She was nervous now, and anxious, tight with the strain of time. Time was everything now. She could almost hear the seconds ticking off. Again she jumped for the ball. Again the guard got it, but this time Karin felt the force of a blow on her arm.

The whistle blasted the game to a stop.

"Personal foul. Berglund take it."

She walked toward the foul line. She had one shot, one shot to tie this game. She felt dizzy, lightheaded. Dots swam before her eyes. She caught the ball as the referee tossed it to her, shaking her head to clear the mist from before her eyes.

I can't see! her thoughts screamed louder than the shouting from the stands. I can't even see the basket.

Then suddenly, as quickly as the dizziness had descended upon her, it was gone. Her head cleared. There, there was the basket, that metal rim up there. All she had to do was heave the ball once, in a perfect arc, and the score would be tied.

She hefted the ball, shifted it, spread her feet, took a deep breath. She held it for that split second. Then she let go, a high looping shot that went clean through.

There were roars from the stands. She glanced at the scoreboard: 57–57. Less than a minute to play, and the ball was hers, hers to take out of bounds opposite the foul line.

She tossed it to Mindy. Mindy feinted to Babs and then tossed it to Karin as she ran to the corner. Karin had to get rid of it; the guard made it impossible to shoot. She sent it to Babs. Babs almost lost it.

178

"Hold on to that ball," she heard herself shout. "Hold on to that ball!" It came to her again, from Babs, feeding it to her in the corner. She caught it lightly. Her guard darted this way and that, trying to throw her off, fighting for possession.

Karin shook her off. She dribbled, feinted a pass, then lifted the ball high above her head. She did not have to glance at the clock. She knew there were less than ten seconds of play, because the crowd was on its feet, chanting off the seconds.

"Ten — nine — eight — seven — six — "

Karin took her time. She felt good now, the great swelling exuberance of power and strength. The great joy of knowing that she was able to do what she was going to do. Free, that was it. Oscar had said she would feel this thing tonight.

I'm free, she thought. And I can put this ball in. I know I can.

She sent it looping, high, high, in that graceful arc that cut clear through space, clean, swift, sure.

It teetered in that agonizing second of indecision, then it dropped through for a score.

She glanced at the scoreboard: Westover 57, Rockridge 59.

The place went wild. Roars deafened her ears. She heard Mindy's voice, and Babs's shouting, "We won! We won!" She herself was voiceless, drained, and empty now that it was over. She watched the crowd descend from the stands upon the floor like a human avalanche. She saw faces she recognized, familiar faces, Oscar and Eric Ringquist and his parents and Miss Fletcher and Steve and the whole town of Rockridge with her grandfather leading the parade!

Nothing was clear for a moment. Nothing made sense.

Just deafening noise and confusion. Then the calm voice of a man cutting through the pandemonium, coming to them over the loud-speaker.

"Attention, please. Clear the floor, please, so we can award the tournament trophies. Will the captains and coaches of the two teams come forward for their awards? The winner: Rockridge. Runner up: Westover."

Someone was pushing her, shouting in her ear: "That's you, Karin. You're captain for Carla. You've got to go with Miss Fletcher and get the award."

She felt a tug on her sleeve as she started across the floor. She turned to look into her grandfather's face. It was a happy face, full of triumph, but she saw something else she had never seen before, a kind of pleading to be understood. And suddenly she did understand him, as she never had before.

"Go ahead," he said. "This is the big moment for Karin Berglund." She knew what he was trying to say, that at last he was accepting her for herself, as an individual, completely on her own.

So it was easy to answer him as she did, for she had a new vision, a new perspective, born of this hard-fought tournament. She leaned toward him and spoke in tones only he could catch.

"This is also a moment for Ed Berglund's granddaughter. A real *svenska*, yah!"

He nodded and laughed, and the pleasure in his eyes was worth more to her than the trophy she was going out to get.

CHAPTER 19

THE AIR TERMINAL was crowded on this last day of June, filled with vacation-bound Midwesterners. Karin watched her grandfather as he took care of the luggage, checked the flight schedule, and counted noses to be sure their party was still together. His face was flushed with pleasure for he was never so happy as when he had too much to do.

"Karin, here is your ticket. Mindy, yours. You each better take care of your own," he said.

If there was one person more excited than her grandfather, it was Mindy. She was coming east with Karin for the summer vacation. She was full of chatter even in this difficult time just before they boarded the jet that would carry them back.

"Just think, we're going to stay in New York the first couple of days. I've never seen New York except in the movies. It's fabulous." She was talking to Eric, for the most part. Eric and Mindy had been dating lately. So Mindy had finally got her wish! If Mindy was delighted, Eric's emotion could best be described as bafflement.

Karin watched them. There was a special expression in Eric's eyes when he looked at Mindy, a combination of amusement and incredulity as if he could not believe that this busybody with the bright eyes and cheeks and turned-up nose had happened to him. It had been on the ride back from the tournament, after Karin and Steve had been reunited, that Mindy and Eric had "discovered" each other and paired off. "I didn't really lasso Eric," Mindy told her friends. "I only twirled that rope so close that he had to jump through or break a leg."

Anyway, the friendship had blossomed into going fairly steady and now, with Eric hovering over Mindy seeing that she had everything and didn't lose her ticket, it was clear to Karin that Eric had found another girl upon whom to lavish his " Swedish-uncle " protection.

" She needs it a lot more than you," he once told Karin. " That Mindy is something. How she's ever gone this far without having her nose clipped off is a mystery to me! She's terrible."

But Karin had seen the warmth in his eyes when he said that and she knew that what Eric meant was: Mindy's terribly feminine and at loose ends and a scatterbrain and *someone's* got to take care of her. And I love doing it.

Karin was glad for both of them. Mindy had got the boy of her choice, and Karin would not be surprised if with a little time and a lot of careful handling, Eric might find that Mindy was the girl of his choice too.

She herself was quiet today as she looked around at the other friends who had come to say good-by. The Ringquists were here, and Oscar and Mamie, her grandparents of course, and Carla, Babs, and Deedie had driven over too. There, at the edge of the group were Steve and his sister.

In the dining room of the terminal where her grandfather had given a farewell luncheon, they had needed three tables pushed together. The talk had been lively, mostly about the good times Karin and Mindy would have back in Connecticut where her father and Joan had taken a house for the summer. Now the gaiety had faded out, leaving that embarrassed hush that descends upon people who are saying good-by to one another.

Karin thought she would not be able to stand that agonizing silence a moment longer. Wanting to get away, she said, " I'm going over to the magazine stand."

"But I bought you four magazines already," her grandfather exclaimed.

"I'm just going to look," she said.

She broke from the group and found her way to the stand. Her eyes, unseeing, traveled over the bright covers of the magazines. She heard somebody say: "Hi there. Going my way?"

She turned, seeing Steve. "I couldn't stand it back there," she said. "I hate leaving people. Especially people I like."

"I know. There's only one thing worse than leaving someone you like, and that's meeting someone you wish you didn't have to."

She laughed. This was Steve, flippant, skeptical, poking fun at his world. She couldn't change that ever, and now she didn't care any longer that she couldn't.

She stood there, watching his changing expression, wondering what was going on behind it. With Steve, she could never tell. But he was coming gradually out of his shell, that was certain. She had even got him going to movies, and he had taken her to his class dance this spring. Now that was progress!

"Will you write to me, Steve?"

"Of course. Will you answer?"

"You know I will. What do you want me to write about? The people I meet and the places I go? Or do you want serious letters about the books I'm not going to read?"

"I think I'd like to hear mostly about you, Karin. What you'll be doing, but especially what you're thinking about when you're away from me. You're the most interesting thing you could put in your letters."

It was a surprising answer and she looked her surprise as she said: "Why, thanks, Steve. That's one of the nicest things you could have said."

183

"I mean it. I'm going to miss you Karin. Nothing's going to be as much fun without you." They were crossing back toward the group. He stopped, detaining her, lowering his voice. "There's one thing I've got to say before we catch up with the others. If you meet someone this summer, some boy I mean, and you think he's your own true love, you nab him, Karin."

She was taken aback. Coming as this did on the heels of his warm comments about missing her, this indifference to her interest in other boys disturbed her.

"It's not what you're thinking," he said. "It isn't because I don't care what you do. But a long time ago, I promised myself I'd try not to be selfish any more. And telling you this is part of that, Karin. I don't want to be selfish about you. I don't like to see anything caged, Karin, not a bird or a person. Now do you know what I mean?"

"I think I do."

The voice over the public-address system cut through their talk. "Flight 31 now loading. Will passengers show their tickets at the gate?"

Steve took her arm and whispered. "I didn't say I *hoped* you would meet someone else you'd like better than me." He smiled. "I'll be wishing every moment that you *won't*."

It was the last thing he said to her. They were separated in the flurry of the departure. Karin was caught up in the final moment of rush, of hasty instructions about letters, of tears and hugs and kisses and promises. In all this confusion, Steve did not come near her, but as she turned to enter the airliner, his was the last face she saw, his was the last pair of eyes she looked into.

She sat there, buckled into her seat, watching the activity outside the jet. She was aware of sounds nearby, of the hostess giving instructions about the use of the oxygen masks in case of emergency, of the chatter of passengers,

184

of the unrelenting voice of Mindy beside her.

" I promised Eric I'd write every other day and he's going to write that often to me too. Isn't it exciting, Skeets? Isn't being in love the most wonderful thing in the world? "

Karin was staring out the window, into the distance, at a tall, slender figure of a boy whose hair was very dark. I must keep him well in mind, she thought, every feature of his face, because this mind picture is all I will have to remember him by.

Mindy was busy sorting out the mementos she had brought along, given her by Eric. Her lap was full. She had a small leather portfolio full of snapshots of Eric. She had a fuzzy bear he had bought for her in the terminal. She had his scarf and his class ring and his club pin and at the last moment he had brought from his pocket a tissue-wrapped box, which Mindy had orders not to open until she was in New York.

Karin had nothing to remember Steve by, no tiniest trinket.

" It's silly," he had said. " People who really care have better ways of showing it than decorating one another like Christmas trees."

She was thinking about this as she watched Mindy fuss over her lapful of trophies. Mindy was chattering as she fussed. " Skeets," she said at last, " you haven't answered me since we got on this plane. I don't believe you've heard a single word I said."

" Yes, I did. You said, for one thing, that being in love is the most wonderful thing in the world."

" That's right, I did. Don't you think it is? "

Karin smiled. She patted Mindy's hand without answering. She was thinking, thinking as the jet rose from the ground and headed east, toward her father and Connecticut.

185

But I'll be back here again, she thought. I wouldn't stay away from this place or these people unless I had to. I didn't want to come and now I don't want to leave. Funny, isn't it?

The jet zoomed smoothly through space, only that slight whistle of sound indicating the speed at which they were traveling. Mindy's voice came to her through the hiss of the jet.

"Why, Skeets, I just noticed. You haven't a single thing to remember Steve by. Didn't he give you anything?"

She did not turn toward Mindy as she answered. She was looking out the window through which only unending space was visible.

"Yes, Mindy, he did give me something."

Mindy, eager to hear, bent toward her. "What, Skeets?"

Karin turned and faced her. "It's nothing you can see or put your hands on, Mindy, but's it's something mighty big and important. You see, what Steve gave me is myself."

AMELIA ELIZABETH WALDEN

Amelia Elizabeth Walden was born in New York City but moved at an early age to Connecticut, where she received her high school and college education. She did graduate work at Columbia University from which she holds a degree.

Miss Walden has always been interested in the theater. She attended the American Academy of Dramatic Arts in New York and has been active in off-Broadway theater circles, writing and producing her own plays. Her experience in theater work has also included acting, directing, designing of costumes and stage sets. Her hobbies include interior decoration, fashion and jewelry designing, collecting antiques, and sports.

She has the distinction of being the only woman writer of girls' sports novels. These stories feature basketball, softball, skiing, field hockey, swimming, horseback riding, ice hockey, and tennis. When asked her favorite sport, Miss Walden invariably answers, " basketball," then adds quickly, " with skiing a close second."

Miss Walden lives in Westport, Connecticut. Before devoting her entire time to free-lance writing, Miss Walden

187

taught in the public schools, and from this contact has gained her special insight into the feelings and problems of young people. She is well known for her books for teen-age girls, and also writes fiction for adults.

In the writing of A Boy to Remember, Miss Walden is realizing something she has long wanted to do: set a novel in a locale outside New England. She has visited the Midwest several times — her husband was a native of Iowa — and always returned with the feeling that Midwesterners were among the warmest and friendliest people she has met anywhere. Miss Walden has touched also upon two other favorite topics of hers, art and Swedish-Americans. "At present half my friends," she says, "are either of Swedish descent or are artists, and some, like the one to whom this book is dedicated, are both!"